Last Days of the Cross

Last Days
of the Cross

Joseph Ridgwell

Ternary Editions
New York

Cover design is by Martin Appleby.

SECOND EDITION

The first edition of *Last Days of the Cross* was published in 2009 by Grievous Jones Press (U.K.)

ISBN-13:   978-1-937073-77-0

TERNARY
EDITIONS
29 Sugar Hill Road
North Salem, NY 10560

www.ternaryeditions.com

CONTENTS

*This book is dedicated to anyone who
knew me in my Kings Cross days*

ONE.

Sydney, Kings Cross. The main drag of Darlinghurst Street. The gigantic electronic Coca-Cola sign. The Pink Pussy Cat. Playbirds International. The Goldfish Bowl. The Bourbon and Beefsteak. And finally the odd El Alamein fountain, fashioned in the shape of a dandelion. Finding somewhere to live was the main priority and I knew just the place to go - the Oakwoods - a budget boarding house, three storeys high, owned by a decrepit landlord.

This dive was on the corner of Roslyn Street and Ward Avenue and on arrival I had second thoughts about the idea. Phew, what a dump. No redeeming features, in fact an eyesore. I paced the street studying the crumbling edifice with the eye of a sceptic. Maybe there was some place else I could stay? Then I remembered my financial situation. $1500 Aussie. That's all I had to my name - not much by anyone's standards and whatever it lacked in aesthetics the Oakwoods made up by being dirt-cheap.

I stepped inside. The Reception was empty. I looked around, picked my nose and scratched my balls. Then I saw the bell and gave the thing a hit - a flamboyant smack. It rang out loud and clear and there he was - the landlord - one Mr Hillwood.

'Ow can I help, mate?' asked the landlord in a way that indicated that he never wanted to help anyone for as long as he lived.

'I'm looking for a room.'

'Singles are $150 a week, plus one week's deposit.'

I did a rough calculation. A week's room in that dump would leave me with little under seven hundred bucks. Hard times - maybe even desperate times but in times like these the most important thing was a roof over the head. Four walls. That's all an aspiring poet needed. With four walls to protect him, he could take on the world.

'I'll pay for two weeks, plus a week's deposit,' I replied like a big-shot.

Hillwood wasn't impressed.

'Rent must be paid each Friday, cash or cheque. A week overdue and ya out,' he sneered.

On the way to the room Hillwood told me the house rules. Every sentence started with the word no. No smoking in the hallway, no parties, no bringing people into the rooms late at night, no loud music, no criminal activity, no drugs, no disturbances, no fighting, no politics. No, no, no and then more no. That's the house rules but there are also the pool rules,' he added mysteriously as he led me to the garden area.

Outside, all was revealed. The alleged garden, a small patch of land bordered by a rickety wooden fence, topped with concentration camp-style barbed wire. In one corner a triangular washing line, in another a rusty barbecue and in another an outdoor toilet. However, none of these features caught the eye, for slam bang in the middle of this miniature wasteland was a swimming pool, the inviting waters shimmering in the Australian sun.

I blinked my eyes to make sure I wasn't imaging things but freakily, the kidney shaped pool even possessed a Jacuzzi. As I stared in wonder, Hillwood proceeded to tell me the pool rules but it was the same shit as the house rules. No this, no that. I didn't pay him any attention and instead pictured jumping into the coolness of the water at the end of another hot Australian day - a cold beer situated at poolside. Then Hillman handed over a rusty key and told me to enjoy my stay. A nice word after all that.

TWO.

I liked my furnished room. It was small and cosy and all mine. There was a single bed, sleeping bag, sash window, set of drawers, mirror, dusty radio, free-standing wardrobe, a stainless steel sink stained with age, a one ring cooker and an ancient bar fridge.

I leaned out of the window. The corner of the street was empty, but later that evening it would be occupied by two or three junkie street hookers, looking to raise enough cash for their regular fix.

As it appeared an artistic thing to do, I decided to observe these girls from the vantage point of my window. I would observe which type of men went with them, how many clients they had, what sort of hours they worked. I would have graphs and tables. It would be a project, an anthropological study.

Still, writing only of prostitutes was too narrow a field. I'd need to diversify - write about all the other characters inhabiting the Cross, the street kids, drunkards, junkies, homeless, the lost, lonely, marginalised and dispossessed. Yes, this was my duty and would surely make my name: Ridgwell - the Bard of Kings Cross.

It seemed like a noble thing to do and the powers that be were bound to put my face on the back of a bank note, or attach blue plaques to all my old residences, my childhood home turned into a museum by the 'Ridgwell Appreciation Society.' There would be guided tours of the Cross - of all my old stomping grounds.

'Ridgwell drank in this bar, sat on that very stool - his favourite tipple a schooner of Toohey's New. Now, it was on this very corner that the legendary working girls of Ridgwell's eloquent prose plied their dubious trade...'

I settled down to write my first Kings Cross poem. I plugged my laptop in and stared at a blank white screen. But what to write about? Twenty minutes later I was still wondering. I ran my fingers along the keyboard, caressing the buttons like they were precious jewels. Then I typed my name and a title: Beach Poem 1, draft 1.

That was it. Forget about ladies of the night and misfits and concentrate on nature. The beach was a good place to start for everybody loves the beach, despite the uncomfortable nature of sand and the burning sun and jellyfish and sharks and the saltiness of the sea.

I'd become a Beach Poet. One hundred poems about the beach! After that I'd become a Cloud Poet, one hundred poems on the clouds, after that a Tree Poet and so on...

Or maybe I should devote my talent to just one subject. Yes, that was it - one subject. How insane yet truly poetic! I considered the ocean, the vastness of that great body of water and the majesty of the roaring waves. Why, the ocean provided the poet with enough material all by itself.

I thought about the sea, the surf, the endless pounding of the beach, the mighty whales and beautiful coral reefs, the storms, the tsunamis. And then there were dolphins, another interesting subject for the aspiring poet. I could easily spend the rest of my life writing about those intelligent marine creatures.

Three hours later I was still staring at a blank white square. Exhausted, I switched the computer off and collapsed into bed. The long flight from England had caught up with me and I was soon slumbering in the sweet arms of Morpheus.

THREE.

When I awoke, the room was dark and through the window stars flickered in a southern sky. Had I dozed off? I checked the alarm clock. It appeared I'd lost an entire evening to sleep. Jet lag, I reasoned forcing myself from the bed.

I gazed into a mottled mirror above the sink. My reflection looked older and I wondered if long haul flights could age you. I brushed my teeth that were covered in a thick layer of fur. Transmeridian fur.

I looked out of the window with clean teeth. The streets were empty. Then I spotted a street walker, a hooker. I grabbed my notepad and jotted down a quick description.

Tall - skinny - long blond hair - arms folded across her chest - cleavage showing - not much tits - now smoking and standing under the yellow glow of a streetlamp.

I threw myself onto the bed and smiled, sagely. This woman would be the subject of my first poem and I had a title, 'The Blonde One Walks A Lonely Street.' I read the title back. It was a little corny but that was okay, until I thought of something better.

I propped myself up against the headboard of my single bed and tried to compose a poem about this blonde street walker...

I woke to a grey, dusty morning of complete indifference. It was was early September - the begining of spring and relatively cool. The sash window of the room was half open and every so often a cool breeze lifted the tattered and yellowed curtain.

I was now refreshed and revitalised; my body clock having returned to some sort of normality. The need to get energised and get my new Australian life into some sort of order was of paramount importance. I grabbed a pen and a scrap of paper and complied a 'things to do' list.

Grocery shopping
Stock up on booze
Write Poetry
Look for work

When finished I gazed at the list and crossed out 'Look for work.' I figured there was enough cash to last a couple of weeks without any need for job hunting. Hopefully in that time I could produce first drafts of around forty or fifty poems.

I grabbed my toiletries and made my way to the communal bathroom. The boarding house was deserted. Good. Most of the other residents were at work slaving their guts out to make some other mug rich. The fools. Not I. Oh no - I was an artist, a bohemian, a man of letters.

The bathroom was a revolting sight. The shower disgusting - the tray covered in a layer of mould, ingrained dirt and the scum of a million other showerers. A man could get a verruca just by looking at the thing. I gagged, held the wall to steady myself, and got out of there.

Annoyed, I made my way to the landlord's room and gave his door a loud and impudent rap. No answer. I knocked again, in fact banging on the door, still no answer.

I rushed to my room and wrote Hillwood a hurried note. I didn't hold back. Those shower trays were disgusting, obscenely unhygienic, an insult to every paying tenant. If they were not cleaned within a day, the local sanitation department would get to hear about it, I warned. Then I pushed the note under Hillwood's door, unsigned; a precautionary measure but the old goat would get the message.

After that, I showered, gingerly, making sure to wash my feet in the sink afterwards. Then I headed off to the supermarket to buy some groceries.

Outside, the sun was shining and the sky was blue. I walked along with a spring in my step. Some days you wake up with more energy than others and this was one of those days. I felt great. This was it. A new start; a new country; a new city, and I was there to achieve something worthwhile, something eternal.

I walked along Roslyn Street and up into the main drag. There were two supermarkets nearby, Riteway and Coles. Coles was the larger food emporium but its prices were notably higher than Riteway.

As I stood on the corner of Roslyn and Darlinghurst im-patient shoppers barged past, forcing me out of the way. And then I saw her for the very first time. Rosie. Although back then, I didn't know her name. She was just a face in the crowd, but not just any face. No, she stood out like a shimmering vision with everything a blurred, grainy backdrop as soon as she hove into view.

She was an Aboriginal girl with long legs and mad hair, dressed like a hooker - tight mini-skirt, torn fishnet stockings and a low cut tee-shirt. She walked fast, pushing people out of the way, like she was on a mission. I decided to follow her. I don't know why - it was an impulse - an overwhelming urge. I crossed to the other side of the road and ran along the main drag. I want-ed to see her face again, to check I wasn't imaging things.

Soon I was well ahead. I stopped outside a strip-club and struck a casual pose. Within seconds the strange girl was in sight and no, I hadn't imagined things. She was stunning; not classical-ly beautiful but oddly beautiful, quirky. She had blonde highlights in her crazy hair and sported an over-sized plastic necklace around a scrawny but elegant neck. Her skin was honey coloured and her eyes were blue. It was the eyes that did it. They were so brightly blue. Almost unnatural.

Within seconds she had swept past me but I kept an eye on her until she disappeared out of sight. Then I pulled a notepad from my shirt pocket and wrote down a quick description.

Another subject for my poetry, I ruminated, another muse - the teenage aboriginal junkie with the blue eyes. I could easily write a thousand poems about that girl. Fifty on the eyes, alone! I thought about those long, dusky legs, her breasts - easily a handful - and the ripped fishnet stockings. It was too much.

I had things to do and tried to put any thoughts of the fascinating girl out of my mind. I headed to Coles supermarket, situated underneath an electric Coca-Cola sign that dominated the southern end of the main drag.

I walked up and down the food aisles wondering what to buy. I would have to budget - stock up on non-perishables and essentials. I began chucking tins into my trolley, one after the other. Then I added a few bags of rice, bread, butter, milk, sugar.

I had everything needed to survive a couple of weeks without requiring any further expenditure. It was a big shop. I headed to the checkout area and waited in a long queue. Apart from some booze, I was fully stocked up. All I had to do now was plot up in my room and write some poetry and with a full stomach and a few beers that would be easy.

Whilst waiting in line, my thoughts returned to the aboriginal girl. I wondered what she did to get by and whether she was a prostitute or a junkie. It was odds-on that she was both but you can never tell. Maybe that was her everyday attire - retro-glam hooker chic, and as I made my way to the Oakwoods I couldn't stop thinking about her.

FOUR.

Hillwood was in his usual position, squatting outside the entrance with a mug of tea in his bony hand. On seeing me, he smiled a gruesome smile.

I remembered the note and immediately wished I hadn't sent it. What a crazed, impetuous fool I was. Okay, I hadn't signed the thing but Hillwood was bound to know. Ah well. I'd have to blag it. I smiled a plastic smile.

'Hi,' I said, nervously.

The landlord cocked his head to one side like a vulture. Then he spat into the gutter, a simple act, which disgusted me.

'I don't want any trouble here mate, d'ya understand?'

Once in my room, I forgot about Hillwood and excitedly unpacked all my groceries. Within seconds the shelves and space beside the one- ring cooker were crammed with food stuffs. I lined up all my tins, labels facing outwards and admired them. Such bright colours and appetising pictures of sustenance, such shiny silver tops.

Plenty of food there, I told myself, enough to last a siege. Writing would now be easy. With a full stomach I'd be able to compose epic poems with my eyes shut! All that was left was to get booze. Yes booze - for the poets of the world must have booze if they've got any integrity. I remembered Li Po and Omar Khayyam, not to mention Dylan, Bukowski and the rest of the poetic pissheads.

I walked to the nearest bottle shop and brought a crate of their cheapest beer, a packet of twenty-five cigarettes and a box of matches. I was now well and truly sorted because all a man needs in the world is beer and food and maybe once in a while a beautiful woman for the night. Ah, happy days!

I took great joy in filling my tiny fridge with beer. I looked at the bottles stacked on top of each other and felt well off. Suddenly I was ravenously hungry. I hadn't eaten anything since my arrival in Australia two days ago. I opened a loaf of bread and made four Vegemite sandwiches. I wolfed down the bread and cooked two tins of baked beans on my one ring hob, eating them straight from the pan to save on washing up.

After dinner I lay on the bed and daydreamed. Through the window an army of clouds raced across an azure sky. An hour later I was still lying on my bed but no longer cloud-watching. Instead I was staring at my laptop with a concerned expression.

I jumped from the bed and sat in front of the machine. Now was the time to write. To create my first Australian poem! I zoned in on the white screen but my mind was a blank canvas, devoid of ideas, inspirationally bankrupt. The white square on my screen never changed, it remained the same, just a blank square of nothingness.

One hour went by, then another and then another. I stood up and glared at my laptop accusingly. So you think you can defeat me, eh, you inanimate technological object? You think you can get one over on the world's greatest living poet, ha, you mug. Can't you see the odds are stacked against you?

At some point, I awoke hunched over the machine with an acute pain in my lower back. The screen was blank, apart from a Microsoft logo moving in diagonal directions. I didn't like that Microsoft logo, it oppressed me and I hit the return key. And there it was - that fucking white screen, proudly defiant, mocking and belittling me with its undoubted victory. I felt crushed.

I closed the laptop. It was late afternoon and the great poet had fallen asleep without writing a word. I opened my little fridge and grabbed a beer from within. After downing the beer in four gulps I decided it was no good shutting myself up within four confined walls. I needed to go for a walk and get some fresh air. I needed to do something. I grabbed another beer and headed into the Cross.

Outside the streets were quiet, the sky a dull grey. In the daytime, the strip clubs and bars of Darlinghurst Street looked out of place like they didn't belong there. The night was when they came into their own. Yes the night, the night, always the night but it wasn't the night - it was daylight and everything looked dead.

I passed shops and bars and faces in the street. I didn't even know where I was going but kept walking until I came to the El Alamein fountain. It was switched off. I sat down and supped my beer, keeping my eyes peeled for any cops for it was an offence to drink alcohol on the streets. Laws. I hated the things. No drinking on the streets - what was the world coming to? But just like the rest of the world, the Cross was changing.

I headed to the McElhone Stairs. At the top of the staircase I gazed at a view of Sydney that spread out before me. From this vantage point I could see for miles in each direction, another great metropolis of the world - home to four millions souls.

I raised my arms to the sky. Surely this city would inspire me to write something truly great! Surely these streets, these people, these Australian visions would enable me to produce the great work I was convinced was within me!

I descended the staircase, worrying and fretting about the future. Had I been deluding myself all along? I mean, who was I to think I could write? Why hadn't I stayed at home and gone to college and studied for something concrete like a career? Why, why, why, because that sounded like hard work and boring hard work, that's why. Hmm, there was no way of avoiding it. I was a fake, a charlatan, a daydream believer.

At the bottom of the staircase, I crossed Cowper's wharf, past Harry's Café De Wheels and walked straight into the public bar of the Woolloomooloo Bay Hotel. I ordered a schooner of VB and sat there watching bubbles rising in the glass.

I wondered what my next move would be but there was nothing to do, so I just sipped my beer and stared into space. The bar was mostly empty and all the customers, including me, looked like they were waiting for something to happen. By the looks of things, it would be a long wait.

After downing the schooner I decided to make something happen by visiting the nearby Art Gallery of New South Wales. Yes, that was it - art. The creative spirit captured through the ages would surely inspire another artist? I waved goodbye to the bartender and left the hotel with renewed enthusiasm.

There was no entry fee for the general areas of the gallery and I wandered around, taking in exhibitions, observing people, keeping my eyes peeled for any possible muses. Some girls interested in art perhaps, or maybe a rich benefactor keen to help out a struggling and penniless artist.

But what lay around the next corner wasn't a rich benefactor but a large oil painting - The Sons of Clovis II, by the French artist, Evariste Luminais. I was in the European section when I saw it and twenty minutes later I was still staring at it. I'd never heard of the frog but the subject matter fascinated me. Two young men with bandaged feet, cast adrift on a small raft, abandoned to their fate. They were lying under blankets looking as pale as death. In the absence of their father, King Clovis, the boys' mother, the Regent Sainte Bathilde, had cut the tendons in her own sons' legs as punishment for their rebellious ways. How cruelly magnificent!

I pulled out my notebook and wrote down a title for a poem, 'Ode to the Sons of Clovis II.' It seemed like a good topic to compose poetry about, even classical in its scope. I found a large leather settee and put pen to paper. An hour later I was still there and all I had was a title. Then, when gallery security began giving me half-concerned looks and stares, I decided it was useless and left in a downbeat mood.

FIVE.

The next few days passed obscurely - uninterrupted periods of sustained creative inactivity, followed by long walks around the city that were equally uncreative but physically beneficial.

Sometimes I locked myself in my tiny garret and settled down in front of my laptop but nothing would come, and hours were wasted trying to conjure up inspiration.

Then the nightmares began, a white screen - an evil beast intent on my destruction - chasing me into valleys, up mountains and across oceans without respite.

I took to staring out of my window for long periods, watching the street prostitutes, jotting down descriptions but creating nothing that could be called 'literature' - poetry or prose. Most days I lay in bed until the early afternoon revelling in my idleness and becoming a slob.

Often I lay farting under the covers, lifting the sleeping bag each time and taking great satisfaction at the stench emanating from my own body. I also masturbated a great deal, until I could masturbate no more, the floor of my room littered with tissues.

I avoided the other tenants in the boarding house as much as possible. I didn't want to talk to anyone. It hardly mattered. Those tenants kept coming and going - one day here the next day gone, aside from the long-term residents.

There was the bearded ex-alcoholic obsessed with washing line protocol. Not unsurprisingly, I'd met him as I hung my washing out to dry. He grabbed me by the shoulder and began an angry tirade. The focus of his ire was tenants who moved clothes from the outside of the washing line to the inside. The clothes on the inside took the longest to dry and people shouldn't do that he warned. I shook free from his crusty grasp, agreeing with him, but making a mental note to always hang my clothes on the outside.

Next door to beardy man was a fat drunken chef. He worked all week and spent the weekends getting pissed on the porch of his room, moaning about his job until he passed out. He was into minimalism. There was nothing inside his room aside from a bed and one chair, which lay on its side, broken.

There were also two lesbian junkies on methadone, one big, fat and ugly, the other small and androgynous, with the face of a weasel. Neither worked, they didn't go out much, they just went to the methadone clinic and lay in bed all day doing whatever it is lesbians on methadone do.

Sometimes I wondered about those residents and ruminated on the poverty of their lives. They didn't seem to do anything or go anywhere. They just existed.

One rainy morning, I counted my money and was alarmed to find my funds running at crisis levels. I hadn't been going out but it was disappearing fast. $350 dollars left. A measly $350 dollars and another week's rent was due.

Mr Hillwood was very efficient in the collection of rent - arrears of more than a week rarely being tolerated. Plus he had never forgiven me for the shower note and would probably evict me at the first available opportunity. Shit. There were no two ways about it - I would have to find a job.

SIX.

The following afternoon I took a walk around the city - a practice that had become part of a daily routine. Later on, I would have another stab at a poem or two and the next day I'd start job hunting. Job. Just that one word was enough to make me shudder!

I left the Oakwoods worrying about the future. Why was life so hard, complicated and gloomy? The sun was shining, the sky a brilliant azure, and yet my world was black. I trudged the streets with legs made out of lead, a dark cloud of depression following me wherever I went.

Eventually, I came to the Andrew Boy Charlton open-air swimming pool. I read the story of Mr Charlton, marvelled at his legendary swimming exploits, and checked out the pool. It was a full size Olympic swimming pool, all lanes, so only for serious swimmers. A few gays sat around sunbathing and preening, apparently more interested in checking each other out than swimming.

I watched the swimmers for a while and wondered if vigorous exercise would inspire me to write. Healthy body = healthy mind. I swore to start a swimming regime and promptly forgot about it.

Next I walked to Mrs Macquarie's chair to check out the views of the harbour. It was early evening when I reached the chair - a stone ledge, cut into a cliff facing the harbour. I sat on the bench and contemplated the pleasures of the harbour, the beauty of the sea, the setting sun.

Tourists came and went, looking at me with accusing eyes. I was in the way of a perfect photo opportunity. Well who cares, I thought. Holiday snaps - how tedious. They'd just have to take the picture with me in it or not all. Most didn't bother but a few did and I was included in several snaps. A couple from Japan, a young family from Ireland and a bunch of old aged pensioners from Geelong.

As night fell, the tourists disappeared, returning to hotels or bars and restaurants, until I was alone. A cool breeze blew. The night contained all the loneliness and sadness in the world. And then stars appeared, one by one, accompanied by a ream of fast moving clouds, dark, mysterious, racing across the moonless firmament. Shivering, I decided to head back to the Cross, to my room and get drunk.

By the time I reached Darlinghurst Street, the evening's entertainment had kicked off. The spruikers were out in force. The neon signs of the strip clubs glowed flamboyantly; the red and white beacon of the coca-cola sign resonated, and cars and taxi-cabs flashed by. As I passed 7/11, a group of juvenile junkies caught my eye. They were all on the nod, leaning here and there, performing miraculous balancing acts.

I crossed to the other side of the drag and continued my observations. The group looked like any ordinary bunch of teen-agers, although rougher and dirtier. I ruminated on the effects of H. At the same age as these kids all I'd wanted to do was move as fast as possible - nothing less than one hundred and fifty miles an hour - not fall asleep on the sidewalk.

I pondered the economics involved. At $20 a bag, heroin was by far the cheapest drug on the streets of Sydney. A schooner of beer was $4. Even a stubbie from a bottle shop retailed at $2. Ecstasy was double the price and cocaine even more. Supply and demand. The heroin was imported direct from the golden triangle of South-East Asia, the cocaine from South America, Africa and Ecstasy from mainland Europe. The transportation costs of importing heroin were far cheaper.

I looked at the kids again. They were out of it. I wondered if heroin could boost creativity and thought of Coleridge sucking on opium and dreaming of Xanadu and of Burroughs and his Naked Lunch. But then there was Trocchi and his downward spiral after Cain's book. Hell, it was something to consider anyway, if I got desperate and needed to find solace in narcotic oblivion.

I wandered into a bottle shop, purchased a six-pack and returned to my grotty little bed-sit wondering if I was suffering from a personality crisis. The Oakwoods was deserted. It was Friday night. Everyone out having a good time or locked in their rooms getting drunk, contemplating their own personal misery in a confined space.

I opened a beer and crashed onto my bed. I powered up the laptop and tuned the battered radio into some random station playing popular hits of the past. Then I poked my head out of the window.

There were no prosties out - still early. I sat back in front of the damned laptop and tried to concentrate. Nothing happened. I opened another beer and then another but it was the same result - absolute nothingness apart from a warm, hazy feeling inside.

I looked into the mirror and waggled a disapproving finger at my sorry-looking reflection. Who the fuck do you think you are - locking yourself away in this shitty room trying to write and going crazy like some latter- day Bukowski or Arturo Bandini? It's Friday night, the night of nights, an evening made for mad lovers and hedonists all over the big city. I downed another beer, winked at my reflection and returned to the Cross, concentrating on putting one foot in front of the other.

In the Goldfish Bowl, I stood at the bar with a schooner of New and a whiskey chaser in front of me. The dive was populated by burnt-out drunks and faded junkies, all in all, a depressing scene. I got talking to an old bum who worked as a security guard. I broached the question of the possibilities of finding work.

He told me to head to the apple orchards in Victoria. After that ridiculous suggestion, I downed my drinks and headed onto the main drag again.

The fresh air hit me immediately and I was suddenly drunk. I wandered into another bar filled with several hundred backpackers - a shocking sight which encouraged me to make a fast exit. Then I wandered down to William Street, past the hookers and trannies, getting several offers of a lady, or an alleged lady for the night.

I found a bottle shop, bought a longneck of Toohey's Red and swigged it from a brown paper bag. Then I saw her again. I hid the bottle behind my back in a desperate attempt not to look like an alki. Why I bothered, I'm not sure because the Aboriginal girl was out of it. She stumbled towards me, offering herself to anyone as she went.

She had on the fish-net stockings, mini-skirt and plastic necklace. We were in front of each other. She looked fucked, swayed, swirled. She opened those blues eyes and my heart burst into a million smaller hearts, which exploded onto the floor in front of her like rose-petals scattered on a forgotten Damascus street eight hundred years ago.

'Looking for a lady?'

'How much?'

'Fifty.'

'What do I get for that?'

'Anything you'se want babes.'

I grabbed a skinny arm.

'Okay, come with me.'

'What tha fuck? There's rooms round the corner, a?'

'Fuck that, I've got a room in Roslyn Street. We can go there.'

The girl stroked the side of her face with one arm. I couldn't work out if she was pissed or stoned, or high but in the end decided she was all three. She looked as if she was trying to size me up or something.

'Where in Roslyn Street?'

'Oakwoods.

'Ah yeah, I knows that. Come on then.'

'What's your name?' I asked.

The girl managed a half-smile and tripped over.

'Rosie,' she said, after re-balancing.

Rosie! Rosie! To my drunken ears it sounded like a wonderful name and she was a wonderful girl - the beautiful girl I'd been searching for my whole life. Okay she was a prostie junkie but who cares? She had to be mine, somehow.

We walked into the Cross, oblivious to our surroundings. The Cross was buzzing - crowds of people thronged the pavements, car horns tooted, the sound of music escaped from bar doors and the night was alive.

I nipped into Mansions bottle shop and brought a litre bottle of vodka, twenty-five Mild Seven and a large packet of cashew nuts. While I waited in a queue I looked anxiously out the window, checking to see if Rosie was still there.

'You'se having a party?'

'Let's boogie.'

'Jeez, you're corny a!'

I was corny but I didn't care, because the girl was walking by my side and all for a measly fifty dollars. Ah, happy days!

Outside the Oakwoods I listened for any signs of life but the whole place was eerily quiet. Good, I thought, as I turned the key. Once inside my room, I snapped the light on and jumped onto the bed. Rosie stood there, shivering and swaying, looking gone. I poured a couple of shots of vodka into two dirty glasses. Standing in the room like that, Rosie made me nervous. I handed her a glass, which she took reluctantly before hiccupping.

'No time to party, mate.'

'There's no need to rush is there?'

Rosie squinted at the contents of the room, visibly unimpressed.

'I need monies.'

I pulled out a yellow $50 note, a pineapple and handed it over. The sight of the cash relaxed her. She downed the vodka and sat beside me.

'Got any smokes?'

I handed her the packet of Mild Seven and a lighter. I studied her as she took the cigarette. What a beautiful girl. To my drunken vision she appeared like an angel of the streets - someone sent to save my soul, to inspire my writing, to talk to in the lonely midnight hour. I downed my beer and opened my laptop. Rosie lay on the bed.

'What's your name, Pom?'

I plugged the machine in and switched it on.

'Joseph,' I replied as I waited for my settings to appear, 'I'm from London. I'd like to write a poem about you, do you mind? I think you could inspire me, you could be my muse, what d'ya think?'

No answer. I looked up. Rosie had fallen asleep on my bed, holding an unlit cigarette in an outstretched hand. I gazed at the strange girl while she slept and wondered if I could love her. What a mad feeling - uncontrollable and completely insane. But I'm always doing that - falling in love too easily, falling in love with the wrong people, always the wrong people - and killing myself.

Then I tried to write a poem, glancing every now and then at the sleeping Rosie. After a few more shots of vodka something happened. It wasn't much but more than I'd managed since my arrival in Sydney all those weeks ago.

Within thirty minutes, I had an entire poem finished - an ode to Kings Cross - a place I'd grown to love as if I were a local. It was my first complete Kings Cross poem, a small miracle in life, a literary beacon of hope. Rosie had inspired me. I stood up and placed my smelly sleeping bag over her. Then I lay down on the floor and closed my eyes.

Kings Cross At 6 AM: Draft I

: Draft I

I walk the dull and dirty city streets around 6 A.M
Sheets of newspaper blown across the pavement
Appear like mad drunken dancers in a crazed musical

The headlined front page becomes a pissed up Gene Kelly
The T.V Listings a gin soaked Frank Sinatra
Hard-faced prostitutes catch taxicabs
Their nights work being done
They return home to fix-up, rest their aching cunts and count the dollars
Two middle-aged hospital workers walk hurriedly, heads bowed to the wind
Preparing mentally to start another ten-hour early shift
The pavements beneath the ATM machines are littered with hundreds of bank receipts
Like the remains of a ticker tape parade celebrating the eternal Saturday night
And a strange listlessness hangs in the air
Like the remnants of energy from ten thousand long gone weekend revellers
The Cross never sleeps
You can grab a beer, a fix and a feed 24/7
But at 6 A.M the place is in a strange flux
Everything animated in a dream like limbo
Drunks stagger along red-faced and glassy-eyed
Junkies, loose-limbed and on the nod, look beat
Then a deluge of brilliant sunshine floods the main drag
And for one exquisite moment everything becomes golden
A frozen moment in time until the gold tide washes away
Replaced by the grey heroin light of early morn
The Cross is steeped in junk history
Echoes of former deals and drug highs reverberate off the club, bar and strip-joint walls
Along with ghostly images of dead prostitutes and doomed drug-addicts
Images that prowl the Sunday morning streets
As I go gliding down through the debauched and exploited decades
Back to a brighter time
When Aboriginal people sat on hilltops overlooking Sydney harbour
Discussing the dreamtime, going fishing and making stencils of their handprints
A million sun-filled days ago

SEVEN.

I awoke in the dark. Something was tickling me. I opened one eye. A large-winged cockroach crawled across my left foot and scuttled away into the shadows.

I was acutely hung-over and my tongue was stuck to the roof of my mouth. I unstuck it and licked my lips. I began to re-member stuff. Drinking in the Cross and Rosie.

I went to get up and hit my head on something hard. It was the underside of the bed. Shit! I rolled out from underneath and jumped up ninja style. Then I scanned the room. My bed was unmade and Rosie was gone.

I jumped onto the bed and sniffed the sleeping bag. I could smell her body odour, a stale, rancid, junkie aroma. I wrapped myself inside the bag and breathed in deep draughts.

Then I remembered my laptop and tore the bag from me. There it was, still on - the Microsoft logo moving diagonally across a black screen. Phew, what a relief. But what about my fast -disappearing wedge? I checked my pockets and pulled out a handful of notes and coins. I counted the smash with shaky hands. $18.76.

Fuck! I collapsed onto the bed and tried to do the math. Fifty to Rosie. Fifty to Rosie. Did I fuck her? No, no way - she fell asleep and then I fell asleep. Well that was fifty dollars down the drain. But where did the rest go? Twenty in the Goldfish bowl, forty in the bottle shop and ten on miscellaneous shit but there should still be two hundred and fifty. Yes, that was it, four fifties, strategically hidden in a pair of socks in the dresser and an emergency fifty in a secret pocket of my suitcase.

I raided the case and pulled out the fifty - relief - then I shot a glance at the dresser. All the drawers were open, with the odd sock hanging here and there. My heart sank. I rummaged through the contents of the dresser, tossing empty socks and pants over my shoulder, until the drawers were empty. The money was missing.

I checked the time. It was eight o'clock. I assessed the situation. I was alone in Sydney with less than seventy dollars to my name. My rent was due in three days and there was hardly any food left. Whatever way I looked at it, I was well and truly fucked - unless I could find Rosie and somehow get my money back.

I rushed onto the daylight streets. Darlinghurst was semi-deserted - a depressing, soulless place in the daytime - the complete opposite to how it looked at night. A Jekyll and Hyde street.

I checked the usual junkie haunts - Hungry Jacks, Mac-Donald's, Barncleuth Square, the El Alamein fountain but there was no sight of Rosie or any junkies for that matter. Undeterred, I headed to William Street and Woolloomooloo but there was no sign of the thieving bitch anywhere. I wandered the back-streets of the Cross in a bemused daze, looking out for love - looking for the girl who had robbed me - but it was a waste of time.

I gave up hope of finding her that day. She was sure to be plotted up in some dirty shooting gallery or junkie pad, spunking my $200. Fucking herself up and forgetting all about me. Well fuck her. We would meet again, sure as eggs were eggs. She wasn't getting away from me that easily.

Dehydrated to the max, I went to 7/11 on Darlinghurst and purchased two Slurpee's. I sat outside Crazy Prices, sucking down the slushes, keeping my eyes peeled for Rosie and wondering what the fuck I was going to do. I needed a plan and a fucking good one. I finished the first slush and started in on the second.

By the time I'd finished both Slurpee's, turning my tongue bright purple in the process, it was obvious what needed to be done. I had to find a job and fast, otherwise I'd be living on the streets.

I went into a newsagent's and bought a newspaper. Then I returned to Crazy Prices and scanned the situations vacant section. There were only two pages of jobs but I was bound to find something. Anyway, the situation I was in, I'd have to take whatever was going - literally anything.

Immediately, I was disappointed. Jobs were few and far between. I scanned the pages several times but all I could find was a job as a skilled labourer and a peanut vendor. I ripped the adverts from the paper and headed to the nearest payphone. I dialled the number for the labourer's job and a tough-sounding Aussie answered.

'Experienced labourer are ya mate?'

'Yeah,' I lied.

'Good with power tools?'

'Yeah,' I lied.

'Okay, turn up for work Monday 8pm, 56 Fisher Street, Petersham.'

I rang the Peanut Vendor job, a man with a French accent answered.

'Any er... experience of selling?'

'Yeah,' I lied.

'We only 'ave weekend work. Is dis okay?'

'Yeah,' I lied.

'Meet me at Manly harbour, nine o'clock, dis Saturday morning.'

With the job situation sorted, I went to the nearest bottle shop and after a thorough search, discovered I could buy a two-litre cask of cheap wine for $9.99. I couldn't afford the dollars but reckoned finding a job, no, two jobs, was cause for celebration.

When I strolled up to Oakwoods with the cask under my arm, Hillwood was squatting outside with his usual mug of tea. He eyeballed the cask.

'Celebrating are we?'

'Yeah, just found a job. No - actually two jobs.'

'Be able to pay your rent on time then, I suppose?'

'Yeah, unless you gonna let me off a week's rent to con-gratulate me...?'

Hillwood snorted into his manky mug and a wry smile appeared on his face, revealing a set of rotted, discoloured teeth.

'Good one mate, ha bloody, ha.'

Before reaching the door, Hillwood called out again but this time his tone was hard and cold. I turned around. Decrepit pointed an accusing finger.

'You know the rules, Pom. No visitors allowed overnight - especially Abbo junkies!'

'Not sure what ya on about Mr Hillwood?'

'House rules are house rules, do it once more and you're out!'

Inside my room, I found a dirty glass and filled it with cheap plonk from the cask. Then I took a big hit. Immediately my throat burned, my eyes watered and I gagged. I shot the remainder of wine in the glass a look of disgust. No wonder it was under ten dollars, pure rot-gut!

Although it tasted disgusting, as soon as the alcohol hit my bloodstream I began to feel good. From then on, I forced the wine down by thinking of anything other than what I was drinking. Sex with two women - toot of wine - sunbathing on a tropical beach - toot of wine - swimming in a turquoise ocean - toot of wine - and so on.

In this way I managed to keep the shit down and as I became intoxicated, the wine began to taste better and better, until eventually it morphed into a magnificent vintage, sourced from the finest French vineyard. After a litre of the rot-gut I switched on my laptop and got down to some serious writing. Drunk and desperate, the poems came easily, one, two, three, four, five, six, seven.

I typed in a flamboyant manner, one handed, drinking straight from the cask with the other. I hit those keys hard, ending each sentence with a fantastic flourish. This went on for about another hour until my burst of creativity was exhausted and my thoughts turned to Rosie and the stolen $200. It was Friday night and she was certain to be lurking somewhere around the main drag, unable to resist the cash opportunities provided by another endless Cross weekend. Figuring she'd be back as soon as her money ran out, I went in search of that crazy Aboriginal girl.

As usual, the Cross was buzzing - the narrow pavements crammed with weekend revellers and party people. Once the fresh air hit me, I was more drunk than in my room and slightly crazy.

I walked up and down the drag several times, searching for Rosie but she was nowhere. I passed bars and strip-joints, glancing at people inside, envious that they could afford to have a good time while I couldn't even buy a slice of two-dollar pizza.

After a while of this, I grew despondent. What if I never saw Rosie again? What if she had moved on to someplace else - Melbourne or Brisbane perhaps? A street kid with no permanent base, wandering from one fix to another, until she grew too old for that kind of life or died.

But what did I care? Really? What was wrong with me? She was a junkie and a prostitute - not the kind of person you would ordinarily view as potential girlfriend material. And on top of that she had robbed me, without a second thought to what might happen to me afterwards. But, of course, that was why I had to see her again - to get my money back. Oh, fuck it!

I walked into an adult bookstore and spent some time flicking through its large collection of porno mags. I found one on bestiality. Colour spreads of a guy fucking a goat, a girl blowing a dog and a really sexy blonde girl fucking a horse! What the fuck!? The horse cock was massive but the girl had it right up her. Jesus! I flicked through some more pages. The kinky subject matter was strangely fascinating and made me hot.

After a while, the guy behind the counter - a young dude with long greasy hair and a patchy beard - began watching me. He could probably tell I didn't have any money and was just bumming around but there was no law against browsing.

At the back of the shop were several cubicles, inside which you could watch porn at two dollars a pop. I stepped inside one and sat down on a stool in front of a blank screen. I didn't even have two dollars. I thought about the girl fucking a horse and immediately got a massive boner. I mean, think about it, shagging a horse. What was the world coming to? I swivelled around on the stool and saw a pack of tissues and a wastepaper bin over-flowing with other used tissues. Nauseated, I run out of there.

Outside the streets bustled with people; junkies, hustlers, gangsters, pimps, bikies, prosties, drunks, backpackers, tourists, and subbies - both Eastie and Westies - the affluent and the poor walking shoulder to shoulder (one of the few times they would be in such close proximity to each other).

I did one final scout of the main drag in a last attempt to find that thieving Aboriginal girl but my search was in vain. Resigned to the fact I wasn't going to find Rosie I retreated to the Oakwoods, drank the rest of the rotgut vino, and prepared for the first day of work.

EIGHT.

I awoke the next morning feeling terrible. I stood up, shakily and tried to turn off an alarm clock that sounded like an air-raid siren. I reached over and threw it against a wall. It smashed into several pieces, but at least the beeping ceased.

Then I saw the ripped cardboard box and empty wine cask. I picked up the silver foil cask and pressed the button on the tap. A lone drop fell onto my parched tongue. I tossed the cask aside.

It was eight o'clock and there was no time to be messing around. No time for a shower, breakfast or any of that civilised shit. I had to get to work on time.

Ferries to Manly took about half an hour but I didn't know the schedule and had to make my way to Circular Quay. I ran into Kings Cross station at speed, hurdled the barriers and hit the escalators running. Getting out at the other end was easier. At Circular Quay, the barriers were down and I was able to stroll through.

I brought a ticket for the ferry. Twelve dollars return. I boarded the boat with a heavy heart, despite the fact the harbour looked beautiful, the green water sparkling like diamonds in the sunshine. I sat near the stern of the ferry and sunbathed and watched the Sydney Opera House and Harbour Bridge pass by with sad eyes. This was a lovely way to travel to work, but my money situation was desperate and took all possible enjoyment out of the scene. Shit, I should've got a job sooner. I watched several seagulls floating on thermal currents. At that exact moment I would've gladly swapped places with the gulls.

At Manly Wharf the French peanut man was exactly where he said he would be, waiting by the entrance. His long grey hair was tied back in a ponytail and he was smoking a joint.

'You are late,' he said by way of a greeting.

'Only arrived in the country last week. Still getting to know my way around.'

'Don't let it happen again, eh?!'

Once intro's were over the Frog took me to a lock-up underneath Manly Wharf. Inside the garage was a wooden cart, some cooking apparatus, oils, sacks of peanuts, sugar and a large parasol. A sign attached above the cart read, 'Golden Nuts.'

I stood around like an idiot while the man explained what everything was for and exactly what the job entailed. Then he had me wheel the cart to the shopping area of the wharf.

Once everything was set up the hippy gave a quick demonstration on how to caramelise peanuts. As it was a dull and stupid process, I didn't pay any attention. Then, while I daydreamed, my employer showed me how to bag nuts and display them for sale to the public.

Just as I was thinking it would be easy to sell a few bags cash in hand the man revealed how he had numbered each bag so that he could work out exactly how many had been sold and exactly how much commission to pay me. Bollocks, I thought, a tight-arsed businessman hippy. Just my luck!

After more demonstrations on the art of caramelising peanuts, the Frenchman handed control of the operation over to me. Before he left, he looked me up and down.

'Anyway, what is wrong with you eh? You look like shit!'

'Mild insomnia.'

At this, the Frenchie smiled and pointed a finger in the air.

'I ave just the thing for zat my friend,' he said mysteriously, before handing me his half-finished joint. And with that gesture he disappeared, leaving me all on my own.

Once he was out of sight, I lit the shrivelled joint and took three long hits. Despite my hangover or maybe because of it, I felt nothing. I took six or seven longer lugs, until I was down to the roach but still nothing. I flicked the J away, dejectedly. Frog boy must have top-ended it. What a fucker!

My hours were 9.30 – 6.30 and I was to be paid $25 a day, a small commission on nut sales, plus five dollars for lunch. I looked around. The Wharf was deserted. With the tourist season a few weeks away I'd have my work cut out trying to earn any decent money from the gig.

I spent the first hour caramelising nuts. Although Frenchie had given several demonstrations on how to cook the things, I'd paid zero attention and consequently burnt my first two batches. I disposed of the evidence of my culinary failures in the nearest rubbish bin. As I did so, I wondered if the hippy counted every single nut but reckoned that would be taking the art of frugality beyond the limit.

After the third batch, I got the knack of caramelising the peanuts and it wasn't long before I had plenty of bags ready and waiting for any unexpected rush. Then I got bored. The wharf remained deserted. A few old aged pensioners waddled around and a couple of local crazies floated past. I cooked some more nuts and saw a pub.

I fingered the five dollars in my pocket and gazed at the building with thirsty eyes. Instead of receding like normal my hangover had inexplicably intensified. Five dollars was enough for one schooner, which, the state I was in, was almost as bad as having none. Fuck it. I'd have to get through the day without a drink. Anyway I was bound to start feeling better eventually.

Around eleven o'clock six surfer girls approached. They looked to be early to mid-teens. They crowded round my stall and fired random questions in my direction.

As they chattered away I asked them if they wanted some nuts but none were interested. I gave them tasters, tried a lame sales pitch but they just teased me and asked for more freebies. Then I changed tactics, telling them I wouldn't be able to eat if they didn't buy some nuts. And although it was almost true, my own pride encouraged me to make it sound like a big joke. Not eat? Me? Joseph Ridgwell - rebel poet and legendary artist of the future? Who'd have thought it? But then one of the surfer girls, a compassionate soul, took pity on me and purchased a single pack of nuts. One $2 pack between six growing girls! After that, they left and I never saw them again.

Next up a middle-aged man approached the stall in crab-like fashion. He studied the placard above my head for a goodly while. Golden Nuts stood out in big red letters against a white background. The man looked at the sign and then at me. He did this several times until he resembled a demented pigeon. Not knowing how to react I stirred some cold nuts in the copper basin and assumed a blank expression.

'Golden nuts?' said the man.

I nodded.

'They should call em John Howard's nuts, a?'

John Howard was the Prime Minister of Australia.

'Yeah, too right.'

'Selling many?'

I waved my arm in the general direction of the empty wharf. The man stuck a hand in his jeans and groped around for some change.

'Give us a couple of $2 bags.'

I handed over the nuts and took the cash. Hey-hey! Things were looking up, six dollars in a little under two hours. Bring it on!

Around lunchtime an unexpected rush of customers descended onto my stall and I took over fifty dollars in five minutes. I cooked two more batches of golden nuts. In fact, I began to sweat from my nut selling and cooking exertions. Then I thought about my own lunch. The hang over of death was still with me, along with the desire for a hair of the dog. I gazed at the nuts in the pan. I could eat some for lunch and wash them down with a schooner in the pub. I grabbed a handful of nuts from the copper basin, lobbed a few in my mouth with a casual insouciance, and went on a reconnaissance mission.

I sussed the layout of the pub. One large bar, one bored looking barmaid, two old timers and six or seven pokie machines. There was also a big window overlooking the wharf. I strolled over to the window. My stall was in full view, exactly what I'd been hoping for. I rubbed my hands together, spun around and marched to the bar. The barmaid, relieved to have something to do, smiled broadly.

'What can I get ya?'

'A New.'

The beer was four dollars. That left me with one dollar. There was nothing for it but to play the pokies. I walked over to the machines and picked out a favourite: The Leopard. I dropped the coin in and went to push one-cent play but somehow pressed one dollar play by mistake. As the reels spun, I cursed. Instead of one hundred plays, I would now have only one.

Then a minor miracle occurred. The feature came up first spin. I pressed play again and like magic, the feature reappeared. Lights flashed and tinny music blared. I didn't need to do anything except watch as my one lonely dollar morphed into one hundred and fifty of the fuckers.

I was rich! After signing for my winnings with the surprised barmaid, I bought another schooner, tipped the girl and returned to my observation point.

The wharf remained empty, the stall abandoned. With the freakish win on the pokies and two beers inside me, my hangover had all but disappeared and life was once more worthwhile.

I sat looking out of the window, not believing my luck. I considered letting Rosie off the $200 and telling her when I saw her next. After my third schooner a large group of people wandered into the wharf. A club outing of some sort.

Energised by the booze, I returned to the stall and cooked up another batch of nuts. Then I walked around the wharf, offering tasters to potential customers. The assertive tactic worked and I began selling nuts. I even thought up a catch-phrase, 'Don't be shy, have a try,' which worked like a treat.

I talked and laughed and cracked jokes about John Howard's nuts. People enjoyed the enthusiasm and responded. Instead of buying one pack of nuts they brought two. My stall became a talking point and the future appeared rosy. No longer would I be Joseph Ridgwell, the Bard of Kings Cross but Joseph Ridgwell: Peanut King!

Despite my win on the pokies, I didn't buy any food but kept eating nuts until I felt sick. Then I popped into the pub for another schooner. The barmaid asked what I was doing and I told her about the stall. She found it funny and told a couple of regulars of my antics. Now I was a talking point.

The afternoon passed in a flash and by the end of the day I'd sold plenty of nuts. At six-fifteen I dismantled the stall. At six -forty-five the hippy was nowhere to be seen, and it wasn't until five to seven that the French git turned up, mumbling something about traffic jams and unavoidable hold-ups. I handed over the day's takings. After counting them several times and checking the numbered bags the hippy was indeed impressed.

'Not bad, Pommie. I think you good, no?'

I shrugged my shoulders. With the beer buzz fast wearing off, I was feeling jaded and deluded visions of being the Peanut King of Sydney had vanished forever. The Frenchman handed over a small yellow envelope. After tax and other deductions I received sixty-eight dollars, a pittance for the hours and work involved - even if I did spend most of the afternoon in the boozer.

'You can do next Saturday, no?'

My rebel instinct was to tell the old fart to shove his pony job where the sun don't shine but remembering my dire finances, I bit my lip and nodded in the affirmative.

Frenchie handed me a $2 pack of nuts.

'Ere, ave these for ze journey home.'

I walked away feeling like I'd been well and truly mugged off.

After just missing a ferry, a kindly boatman allowed me to board the faster and more expensive Jet Cat at no extra charge: a simple act of generosity that warmed the cockles of my heart. I climbed to the top deck of the catamaran and watched as the engines roared and plumes of white, cascading water jettisoned into the air. It was a chilly night. The other passengers were down below in the warmth.

A large full moon, surrounded by a throbbing corona reflected off the vast body of water. The high-powered catamaran completed the return journey in half the time of the ferry. As we sped under the harbour bridge, wave after wave of fruit bats crossed the darkening Sydney night like a horror movie. Then I remembered it was Saturday night and I'd just been paid. Everything would be okay.

NINE.

I returned to the Cross ravenously hungry. Sick of tinned shit and buoyed by the win on the pokies and my first Aussie pay packet, I found a little Korean takeaway and ordered chicken Pah Jook.

I sat in my room and ate my Korean and drunk a couple of beers. The food was delicious and encouraged me to return for a second helping. Back on the streets, the pavements were buzzing and I weaved in out of the crowds at speed. I also kept a keen eye out for Rosie, like I always did whenever I hit the Cross but, as usual, she was on the missing list. The young girl at the Korean takeaway recognised me the second time round.

'Ooh, you very hungry tonight.'

At the Oakwoods, a few of the residents were hanging out by the pool area, drinking and chatting in relaxed fashion. For once, Hillwood was off the scene. He had gone to stay with relatives in Newcastle and wasn't due back until Sunday evening. I was surprised that the old misery guts had any family but without his killjoy presence around, the atmosphere was far more convivial.

There were three new faces on the scene: two Australians and a pretty Japanese girl. The ex-alki beardy man was pontificating on various boring subjects - mostly to do with Hillwood's rules and regulations, laundry rotas and other pointless shit.

Sat in the doorway of his room, drinking beer, like he did every weekend, was the fat chef. His face was bright red and for once he wasn't moaning about his job but was in a genial mood. His supervisor had been sacked for unauthorised use of petty cash and the cause of all his suffering was out of his life forever. The new supervisor was a little beauty the chef kept repeating: played it hard but fair.

I sat next to the Jacuzzi and ate the rest of my Pah Jook. The Aussies gave the pretty Jap bird a rudimentary language lesson. She repeated each learned word in exaggerated Pidgin English before bursting into hysterics. The irritating girl was also flirting outrageously and the Aussies - two feral looking dudes, fresh in from the Blue Mountains - couldn't believe their luck. And believe me, neither could I.

I concentrated most of my observations on the unlikely trio, while every now and then fielding dumb questions from Beardy and the drunken but happy chef. Everyone stayed around the pool, drinking late into the night: all except the ex-alki who stuck strictly to juice. At some point, the Aussies and Jap girl disappeared, giggling up the main staircase, taking most of the energy from the party with them in the process.

An hour later the party was all but over but after another visit to the communal toilet I found Beardy Man waiting for me outside.

'Can I trust ya?' he whispered mysteriously.

'Huh?'

'To keep quiet about something interesting?'

Now I was confused. What the fuck? Beardy looked at me and I looked at Beardy.

'Follow me,' he whispered.

'Where to?' I whispered back.

'To the roof!'

Fuck it, I thought. Maybe he's got a telescope up there and I'd always fancied doing a bit of stargazing.

'Okay, let's go.'

Up on the roof, Beardy adopted a conspiratorial air. He walked to the edge of the roof, knelt down and peered over the parapet. I noticed some stars flashing in the sky but no telescope.

'Jeez, will you look at that?'

Now I was curious. What was he looking at? I walked over. Beardy turned around and pressed a finger to his lips.

'Keep quiet.'

I knelt beside Beardy and peered over the edge. Way down below were several apartment windows. One of the windows had no curtains and with the light on, we could see right inside.

The two Aussies and the Japanese girl were lying on a bed stark naked. Immediately I got a hard on. The three were passing a large bong between them. After a few seconds of this, I pulled away and looked at Beardy. He was engrossed in the scene, pure voyeurism, a bona fide Peep freak. I thought about my room. Nope, nobody could peer into it unless they were suspended fifty or sixty feet in the air, and without the help of a crane, an impossible feat.

'Listen, don't get me wrong kid.' said Beardy, 'I don't go around peeping into people's rooms. It's just the other day, I was up here fixing the T.V aerial and I saw them at it. It was purely by chance.'

'No worries mate. It's their fault for not drawing the curtains.'

'Yeah, it's like they want someone to see.'

'Maybe they're into dogging.'

'What's that?'

'You know, when people like other people watching an' shit.'

'Do people really go around doing that sort of thing?'

'Of course. Look, now they're doing a spit-roast!'

'Jeez!'

After both Aussies had taken a turn on the Jap, I started to get cramp from the crouching position and was also busting to swerve to the privacy of my room and bash one out.

'Listen, I'm going back to me room,' I told Beardy.

Beardy waved me away with an inpatient arm.

'Yeah, yeah, no worries. But remember this is our little secret. Right kid?'

I touched the tip of my nose twice.

'Mum's the word.'

After the free sex show, I was horny. Images of the two young Aussies fucking the obliging Japanese girl flashed through my mind, fanny on cock, cock in mouth, different positions and other pervy stuff. I was also jealous. Why did some guys have all the luck? Then it dawned on me. I hadn't had a shag since coming to the land of the Kangaroo. This was a depressing situation that needed to be remedied and without delay. I set off for the main drag at a furious pace.

TEN.

The main drag was strewn with weekend revellers. Drunken people reeled along the sidewalk, exited and entered bars, strip clubs and restaurants. At that late stage of the night, the crowds had begun to thin out, and the streets were populated with groups of stragglers.

I was drunk but didn't care and hurtled along at a tremendous pace, oblivious to everything and totally focused on my mission to obtain the services of a prostitute.

I headed to William Street where the street hookers - the least expensive of all working girls - plied their trade. I took a short cut along Victoria Street but became disorientated and walked in the wrong direction, passing the McElhone stairs in the process.

Realising my drunken mistake, I doubled back. On reaching the staircase again, lo and behold, there she was, sitting four steps down with a gang of junkies. Rosie - the one and only. The kids were on a junkie run, rushing madly to the warped heroin death drive beat. Drunk, I didn't even assess the situation and jumped the stairs two at a time before grabbing Rosie by the shoulders.

'Hey, where d'ya go?'

Rosie looked at me with drowsy eyes, recognised me briefly, before pushing my hand away.

'Get tha fuck off me.'

I stood back, swaying. The rest of the gang were now pay-ing strict attention to the situation that had developed. Within seconds a ring of junkie adolescents surrounded me. I prodded Rosie on the shoulder.

'You stole my last $200!'

'What the fucks ya talking about? I don't even fucking know youse.'

'You came to my place in Oakwood's, d'ya remember?'

An anaemic blond kid in need of a good scrub, followed by a decent meal, pushed me out of the way.

'Look, fuck off fella. The bitch says she doesn't fucking know ya.'

I stared at the blonde kid in drunken amazement. The anaemic looking fucker must have been all of 80 pounds and had just called my girl Rosie a bitch, so fuck him. I swung without warning but it was a wild swing - uncoordinated - and I lost bal-ance and fell over.

As I lay on the cold stone floor, the kicks came hard and fast. I curled into the foetal position and tried to protect my head with my arms but it was useless.

During the beating and confusion I could hear Rosie's voice. She was yelling and shouting at the junkie fucks to stop and I wondered if deep down somewhere in the recesses of her soul she cared about me. Just when I thought I was about to be kicked to death, the blows stopped coming and someone rummaged through my pockets. There were forty dollars in one pocket and fifty stuck in the little secret hip pocket. Unable to defend myself, the unidentified assailant located the forty and quickly relived me of the sum.

'Come on. Let's get the fuck outta here.' someone said.

I opened an eye and caught sight of the junkies fleeing the staircase. Rosie was stood there and for a fleeting moment our eyes locked. I spat out some blood and Rosie held a hand to her mouth. There was horror and sadness etched upon her pretty fea-tures and I tried to manage a smile. Then Rosie mouthed the word 'sorry' before she too disappeared into the night.

I lay curled on the stone floor in a daze, before staggering to my feet. I checked my body for signs of injury but aside from a cut lip and aching ribs, I was okay.

I leaned against a wall and caught my breath. Fuck, what an idiot. Was I losing the plot or something? I could've got killed. I remained leaning against the wall for a long time. Funnily enough, although I'd been beaten up and was aching all over, I was happy. Somehow I reckoned Rosie and me had made a connection: one of those rare connections that seldom occur in this world, maybe only once or twice in a lifetime.

This knowledge (which could only be fact) made me feel good. If I could get Rosie alone and tell how I felt, she was sure to feel the same way and then the realisation that we were born to be together would hit us like a holy illumination! God, I felt happy then, safe in the knowledge that I had met the love of my life. Strangely, despite this crazy declaration of romance, an association of thoughts made me think of getting a Brass again. Yes, that's what I needed - a sexual experience without any emotional ties to erase the memory of the beating. I staggered towards William Street.

It was late now, not many people around, just the aimless and the hardcore and those with nowhere else to go but down. Most of the hookers had gone home and the streets were desolate and moribund. I held my aching ribcage and limped into the night.

I saw one outside the Traveller's Autobahn. An Asian girl, strutting her stuff in the shadows, head held high. She reminded me of the Jap girl from the Oakwoods. With that in mind, I approached.

'Looking for a lady?'

'How much?'

'$80.'

I nodded. The prostitute looked me up and down.

'Okay, young boy. You follow me.'

I followed. The Brass took me to a smart block of private flats at the bottom of Bayswater Road. Moments later we were inside a decent looking but dimly lit apartment. The girl asked if I'd like a drink. So far the business of paying for sex had been a civilised affair. I sat back in my chair and relaxed.

'Got any beers?'

The woman pulled a face and tottered to a small kitsch mini-bar, which stood in a corner of the room like a lost artefact from the decade that fashion forgot.

'No beer. That shit make you fat!'

It was then I noticed for the first time how strong her accent was, South-East Asian - possibly Thai or Filipino - but hard to pinpoint exactly.

You like gin & tonic?'

'Fine with me.'

Once the Brass had fixed the drinks, we sat and made small talk. It was the usual intros. Where are you from? What do you do? As we chatted I gave her the once over. She was tall for a slope and skinny, with a small bum and big breasts. She wore layers of foundation, plenty of mascara, lipstick, eyeliner. In fact everything about her was exaggerated. When my drink was half-finished the girl picked it up.

'We go bedroom now.'

Once in the boudoir the girl undressed, revealing black suspenders, bra and knickers. Class, I thought as I dropped my jeans and pants and cast off my tee-shirt. I sat down on the bed. The Brass knelt in front of me and went straight to work.

I was still drunk and despite an effective technique, I was confident the girl would have to work hard to earn her $80 dollars. I slipped a hand inside the prostie's bra and gave one of her breasts a firm squeeze. The breast was solid, like it was made out of cement but I kept on squeezing. The girl stopped sucking and flipped her bra off. The breasts popped out but didn't move. Stone tits. I leaned over and sucked on a nipple but it was weird and unnatural like sucking on a nipple encased inside a wet suit.

After a while of the breast feeling and cock-sucking business, I decided to be more assertive. I slid a hand down to the suspenders and slid a finger inside. The Brass jumped up and her hair slid to one side. A wig.

'You wan full sex?'

'Yeah.'

'You sure wan full sex with girl like me?'

'Yeah.'

The Brass produced a condom and expertly slid it onto my cock. Then she rolled onto her back, undid her suspenders, slid her knickers off and opened her legs. I looked at what was in front of me, a small, limp, pathetic looking cock, shrunken balls and shaved pubic area. I stared at the sight open-mouthed and backed away.

'Where you go?' said the Brass.

I climbed into my jeans and tee-shirt in world record time.

'Listen, I can't do this, I…I have to go.'

The trannie got on her knees and crawled along the bed.

'Come back here young boy, you wan fuck. I thing you wan fuck.'

I slipped into my plimsolls and continued edging away.

'Sorry… can't… got to… erm.'

The trannie pouted angrily.

'You back here now!'

I ran to the door.

'Come back here young boy! Come back now. I demand to be fucked!'

I opened the door and stumbled along the corridor. I missed the lift and found some stairs. Behind me the trannie screamed out like an old hag. I ran and ran, losing myself in a maze of darkened corridors and stairways. I found myself in a gloomy basement, an underground car park. I crawled through an open window and into the outside world. Then I scaled a large wall and dropped to the other side. I landed in a street. Where the fuck was I? I couldn't hear the Brass anymore and all was silent.

Out on the streets I felt disgusted and nauseated. I kept picturing the cock and balls before my very eyes. Freaky fucking shit. Up ahead, the red and white light of the giant Coca-Cola advertisement loomed.

Ah, there it was, the Cross, my home - my place of refuge. I needed a drink and badly. I wandered into the Kings Cross Hotel, bought a schooner and downed it in one. I burped and wondered if what had occurred was a strange, kinky dream. Then I wondered if life was a dream and death our awakening. It could be possible if you believed it was.

My ribs hurt. I ruminated on events. Maybe I should've shagged the transsexual for life experience? What a wimp, running out like that. How rude. No self-respecting poet would've done the same thing. What would Bryon have done, or Rimbaud, Verlaine, Dylan Thomas, Gerard Manly Hopkins, Bukowski et al? Undoubtedly they would've all steamed in, thrown caution to the wind and then wrote about it afterwards. That's why I was unable to write, I just didn't possess the wild and rebellious nature of the true poet. Ah fuck it. What was done was done and when it came right down to it I just couldn't stick my cock up another man's arse. I drank one final schooner and hobbled back to the Oakwood's to forget about everything.

ELEVEN.

I awoke late to the sound of someone calling my name in a dream. I was lying in bed fully clothed. The room was hot, I was sweaty plus I felt like total shit. I tried to get up and groaned loudly, a searing pain from my ribcage. I dropped back onto the bed. Then I heard the sound of my name again. It was the voice of a girl. I forced myself up from the bed and hobbled to the window. I tore the yellow rag aside. The brightness of the sun dazzled my eyes and forced me to squint but somewhere out there was a brilliant blue sky. The voice called out again.

'Hey Joseph. It's me. Over here.'

I tried to follow the sound of the voice. My eyes scanned the street, looking in every direction and then I saw her. She was leaning against a palm tree, smiling and beckoning. It was Rosie and just the sight of her sent my heart into raptures of immeasurable pleasure - all my pain forgotten. I mouthed some words, a broken sentence, meaningless. Rosie's eyes darted left to right.

'Can I come up?'

I rubbed my eyes to check I wasn't imagining things but when I looked again, Rosie was still there, leaning against the palm tree. Can she come up? Of course she fucking could!

Then faded memories from the previous night kicked in. Work; drink, caramelised peanuts, pokie wins, the party round the pool, the free sex show, the kinky trannie experience and finally, more drink.

I also remembered the beating I'd taken at the hands of Rosie's junkie friends; flashbacks of kicks to the body, shouting, Rosie's sad look and her mouthed 'sorry' before she ran away. Fuck her and fuck them. But why was she here? I had to find out what she wanted and then she could go to hell. Anyway she couldn't come in because of old Hillwood and all his stupid rules. Whatever it was she wanted, she would have to tell me right there, out in the street.

Then I remembered that Hillwood wasn't due back from his trip to Newcastle until the evening and the usual house rules didn't apply. Fuck the street, she could come to my room, it would be safer there, just the two of us alone together. That way we could have a proper talk and settle our grievances once and for all behind closed doors.

I signalled for Rosie to wait and headed for the stairs but despite the mad excitement caused by her unexpected reappearance, I was in agony. I came to a rapid halt and began hobbling, holding the rail with one hand and my ribcage with the other. As I descended the staircase, it proved hard to breathe properly and I feared something was broken.

Outside Oakwoods I signalled for Rosie to come over. She skipped across the street, smiling and looking goofy. She was wearing a faded pink wife-beater vest, a pair of blue satin running shorts and ragged white plimsolls. She was naturally stylish, like she didn't have to try.

'Come up to my room.'

Rosie hesitated.

'What about Hillwoods, a?'

'Don't worry. He's not around - he's in Newcastle.'

'Really?'

'Yeah, really. Now come on.'

At that news Rosie flashed me a big dopey smile and for the first time I noticed how big her teeth were: not bucked but large pearly whites. It didn't matter though because there was something strangely appealing about those big teeth, adding to her charms. As we climbed the stairs Rosie noticed my discomfort and held my arm.

'Are youse okay?'

'Yeah.'

Inside my room, I lay down on the bed and tried to make myself comfortable. Rosie remained standing, looking thoughtful and guilty.

'There's a beer in the fridge.'

Rosie grabbed two cold beers. After opening mine and taking a few gulps I felt a little better. Rosie sat on the end of the bed and apologised for the actions of her friends but I wasn't listening.

I told her to stop apologising, that it didn't matter, that it was my fault for throwing the first punch. Rosie laughed and giggled until she reminded me of a kid and I didn't even know how old she was.

'Yeah Pom. You just appeared from nowhere and swung for Frankie but you missed big time, a?'

'Tell the dude he was lucky. If I wasn't so pissed, I would've done the prick. No mercy,' I wheezed and started laughing but the pain was too much and I had to stop. Rosie shot me a concerned glance.

'Let me take a look at those ribs.'

She pulled my tee-shirt up and caressed my torso with soft, gentle hands.

'Do they hurt?'

I felt the hands touching my body and was immediately turned on. The soft skin, the cold, golden warmth. God, how much I wanted to fuck this girl but at the same time it seemed impossible: a violation.

I glanced at my ribs, 'Yeah, they do but I'll be alright.'

'Hey, I's nearly forgot what I came here for.'

Rosie reached inside her shorts and pulled out four folded fifty dollar notes and pressed them firmly into my hand.

'Here's ya monies - the monies I borrowed.'

Borrowed? I looked at the notes in my hand and it tore me up. I was vulnerable and emotional. I took another swig of beer and threw the notes at Rosie.

'Forget it, I don't need the money but it would've been nice if you'd asked first.'

Rosie threw the money back at me.

'Jeez, I think I did ask, didn't I?'

'Yeah I think you did.'

Rosie stood up and examined the contents of the room, eyeing my laptop with interest and acting fidgety.

'So, tell Joseph - jus why did ya come here, all the ways from England?'

I sat up in bed. So far, I hadn't told anyone about my real reason for coming to Australia - about my mad aspirations to write poetry - but Rosie was different from all the rest: a special case. And it might impress her if I told her I was a wannabe poet.

'You won't laugh if I tell you the truth, will ya?'

Rosie sat down on the bed and held my hand.

'No way. I won't laugh. Swears.'

'I came here to get away from London - away from all the distractions - so that I could write poetry. You know, different environments, different inspirations. You see, I aim to be a poet some day and I want to write about the characters of the Cross.'

Rosie looked at me in a different way after that, a more intense way.

'A poet,' she said softly, the words tapering off to nothing.

Then I was embarrassed. Telling someone you want to be a poet in the 21st century sounded absurd, pretentious and hopelessly romantic.

'Hey, d'ya wanna another beer?' I said, changing the subject.

Rosie fetched another couple of bottles from the fridge.

'I's never met a poet before, a?'

I supped on the beer and Rosie told me to put my arm around her shoulder so as to get more comfortable. I didn't need telling twice. It felt wonderful like that just laying side by side, sipping beer in that tiny room in the heart of the Cross, on a sunny Sunday morning.

Then I saw the stains on Rosie's shorts and flinched. Were they what I thought they were? I looked again - crusty grey and white tracks, which had to be semen stains: a gross sight. And where had she been all this time and how did she get the $200? I downed a large gulp of beer to suppress the nausea. It worked.

'Youse okay?' said Rosie.

'Yeah, it's the ribs. How was your night?'

But Rosie didn't want to talk about her night. She wanted to talk about me, London and England and my crazed idea of becoming a poet. She started asking all sorts of random questions about my life, my family and then about almost anything, rambling from one subject to another.

I looked into her eyes. The pupils were massive - entirely obscuring the blue. She was buzzing on something but totally lucid and in control. I reckoned it was an alcohol and amphetamine combo.

I told her bits and pieces about my background - where I came from, what London was like, what jobs I'd done and why I wanted to become a poet.

After that confession I turned the conversation back to her life but she was evasive. The only scrap of information she let slip was that she originally hailed from a place called Matraville, in Sydney's East. Then I asked how old she was and she sighed and yawned a fantastic yawn.

'Nineteen a.'

I took another hit of beer.

'Just a chicken come out of the egg.'

Rosie turned towards me until we faced each other. Our lips were now just millimetres from touching: her warm beer breath wafting into my nostrils.

'Joseph, d'ya wanna be my friend? I think ya crazy a but nice with it.'

I put my hand to her face and gently stroked her cheek.

'Yeah, why not? I'm getting lonely all by myself and maybe we can look out for each other.'

Rosie moved a fraction closer, 'Yeah,' she whispered and her lips opened and her tongue entered my mouth and mine entered hers. Then we just lay there kissing for ages, doing nothing more than that, just kissing, with our tongues and lips touching ever so lightly and every so often not even touching. Rosie slid a hand inside my pants and caressed my hard-on.

'D'ya wanna root?' she asked playfully.

The request took me by surprise and embarrassed me. I moved her hand away. Did I want a root? No I didn't and I don't know why. The hard facts were that Rosie sold her body to survive on the streets. Maybe that's what it was, I wasn't sure but the words emerged from my mouth just like that.

'How much?'

Rosie pulled away from our embrace and punched me on the arm, hard.

'Jeez, I thought youse says we were gonna be friends. Well fuck youse!'

She sat up in bed, facing away from me. I couldn't believe what I'd just said, how cruel and unnecessary. I sat up but couldn't manage it. Rosie was still looking away but I saw her wipe some tears from her eyes.

'Shit, Rosie I'm sorry. I was joking.'

'Get fucked. Why don't you want a root? Don't ya think I'm sexy?'

'Jesus Christ, of course I do but...'

'Too late anyhow. I've gotta be off.'

This time I did manage to sit up - pain or no pain.

'Where ya going?'

'Outta here, that's where I'm going,'

'Hold on one moment.'

'No, I can't.'

'But when will I see you again?'

Rosie slipped into her tattered plimsolls without any laces, like the ones I'd worn when I was a kid during physical education.

'When you've got enough dollars to afford what ya never gonna get,' she said with a sneer, before leaving the room and slamming the door behind her.

TWELVE.

The next morning, found me crammed into a train carriage with a bunch of commuters, headed to a place called Fisher Street in the Eastern suburb of Petersham. To prepare, I'd rubbed a tube of painkiller gel onto my injured ribs and could now walk almost normally, albeit with a more than passing resemblance to a Thunderbirds puppet. Fortunately, Beardy man had kindly given me some written instructions on how to get to Petersham and I'd woken extra early to make sure I got there on time. I stood in a corner of the City Rail carriage thinking about Rosie.

After she'd left my room, I'd hobbled to the nearest bottle shop and pharmacy for a cask of wine and painkillers. Then I sat in my room, supped the wine, popped painkillers, obsessed about the girl and tried to write some poetry. But as usual I was unable to write any poetry. All I did was type Rosie's name over and over on the white screen until in the end I'd typed her name 6,789 times. I know this because I'd used the word count facility.

Then I carved the number 6,789 into my arm with my Swiss Army knife, it was painful but I did it. After that I lay on my bed and masturbated with a bloody arm, imagining myself making love to that beautiful aboriginal girl over and over, as my dick turned red.

Drunk, I stared into the mirror and started a conversation with myself, which went something like this: You think you're a poet, what makes you think you're a poet, has anyone other than yourself called you a poet, who do you think you are calling yourself a poet, what the fuck is a poet? Poet, poet, poet, you ain't no fucking poet! This tedious monologue of negative reinforcement went on for a couple of hours until, exhausted, I crashed out on the bed.

Back on the train I tried to get the thought of Rosie and poetry out of my head by studying the other passengers, suits, cleaners, builders, students, pensioners, ordinary folk going nowhere. I observed well-fed businessmen, career women and office workers, easily subjugated individuals stuck in nine-to-five nothingness forever. No one was talking. Everybody looked blank and an air of desperation permeated the claustrophobic atmosphere. Fuck this shit, I thought languidly as sumptuous images of a naked Rosie floated through my sozzled brain.

I found myself walking along Fisher Street, eyes searching for number 56 or any residence that resembled a building site. As it happened, number 56 turned out to be a large pile, a mansion. Standing on a mangled lawn in front of the house were three burly dudes discussing business. They looked exactly how builders should look - beer-bellies, huge biceps, steel-capped boots, overalls, tool belts, unshaven. I gave myself a quick once over, skinny, shorts, tee shirt and battered plimsolls. Fuck it. I looked like I was going to the beach.

As I approached, the three men stopped talking and eyeballed me. They were twice my size, twice my age and immediately I became self-conscious of my lack of work experience. What was I doing masquerading as an experienced labourer proficient in the use of power tools? Was I off my nut? I extended to my full height and stuck out my puny chest.

'Alright?' I said, cheerily.

One of the men let out a stifled snigger, while the other two looked puzzled.

'Are you Joseph?' Asked a thickset blonde man who sported a Village People style moustache but was in no way camp.

'Yeah.'

'And you're handy with power tools right?'

'Yeah.'

'Kango?'

'Yeah.'

'Okay, follow me Pom.'

I followed. Village People led me to a bathroom and gave me the low down about the job. He was renovating the building, ripping the guts out and making everything new. Apparently, when the project was complete he would sell the place for a tidy profit. I nodded and feigned interest but lucrative or not, property development was a boring and pointless way to make a living.

Once in the bathroom, moustache man showed me the task in hand. He wanted all the tiles taken off the walls. I looked at the tiles and groaned inwardly. Put up many decades ago and stuck to a concrete base - they were the hardest type to get off. Nightmare scenario. Somebody had made a feeble attempt in one corner but had stopped or given up after only two or three of the fuckers had been successfully prised from the wall. Despite my best attempt to conceal it, Village People noticed my look of despair.

'It won't be easy, Pom but it's gotta be done,' he said.

Once I'd been told what to do, the builder disappeared, returning moments later with an industrial drill, the type used to dig up roads and shit, along with a pair of safety goggles,

'And you've used a Kango before, right?' he asked, handing me the drill and goggles.

So that's what a Kango is I ruminated, as I put the goggles on and tried to look like I knew how to handle a drill of such proportions.

'Yeah. Not for a while, though.'

'Okay, well see how ya get on.'

'Will do boss.'

Once Village People had fucked off I assessed the situation. Me, Joseph Ridgwell, the greatest poet of his generation reduced to drilling tiles off walls in a non-descript Sydney suburb.

Somehow things were not going according to my grand Australian plan - not that I had a grand Australian plan to start off with but that didn't excuse the fact that it now lay in tatters.

Then I had an idea. Yes, that was it. I could find inspiration for my poetry amongst the workingman and the working life.

Why write about the ocean and clouds and truth and beauty, when I could write about the reality and nobility of hard graft?

I picked up the heavy drill and waved it around like a gun. Ode to the Kango drill. There. See? I already had a title. Then I glanced around, formed my eyes into slits and smiled wryly. This was reality; this was real life, the day-to-day living, working hard just to earn a crust. This is what makes the world go round. But first I had to do the work that made the world go round, so I would still have a roof over my head come the end of the week. The poetry would have to wait until I got home. I placed the goggles over my eyes and got into position.

I was already sweating by the time I switched the drill on, three days worth of alcohol oozing out of every pore in prodigious amounts. I shoved the butt of the drill into my shoulder, supported my bruised ribs as best as I could and pressed down hard on the trigger. The tremendous noise of the drill reverberated off the bathroom walls and roared in my ears.

Five minutes later, after an extended bout of drilling, I dropped the Kango to the floor and tore off my goggles. I wiped sweat from my brow and gazed at my handiwork. Nothing had happened, not a single tile was off and not a crack had appeared. The drill had only managed to chip some glaze from the tiles and extract some ancient grout. I wiped my brow once more, picked the drill up and roared like a maniac. Then I recommenced drilling.

The noise was deafening, my whole body vibrated and sweat dripped into my eyes and mouth. I cursed and swore as fragments of sixty-year-old tile whizzed around the room like shrapnel. Five minutes later, the tiles remained on the wall - some superficial damage but otherwise intact. I dropped the drill and sat on the edge of the bath. My hands trembled from the exertion and I was breathing hard.

'Must start an exercise regime,' I panted, 'getting outta shape.'

Just as I was about to give it another go with the drill Village People re-appeared. He took one look at the bathroom walls.

'Have ya started yet?'

For a split second I contemplated picking up the drill and doing a Rambo on the cranium of this dolt but the thickness of his skull would've meant the same outcome as with the tiles.

'Those tiles won't budge boss.'

'Let me see how ya doing it, kid.'

I got into position and tried to look professional. Village People cocked his head to one side and wagged a disapproving finger.

'Jeez, are ya sure you've used power tools before?'

I put the drill down.

'Yeah but not for a while.'

Village People took the drill.

'What ya like with a Sander?'

I said nothing.

'Angle-grinder? Router? Circular saw? Tacker?'

'Er, maybe you could give me a quick run-through?'

Village people kicked some tile fragments across the room and let out an angry sigh.

'Ya said ya were good with power tools on the phone mate!'

This prick was getting onto my nerves but I desperately needed to keep the job. I began waffling.

'Er, yeah, sorry an that but I wasn't sure which tools an ya can never tell... Is there anything else? I mean like something with...or but... you know what it's like an so if ya...'

Despite his silly moustache and everything else, this builder wasn't one to suffer fools gladly. He raised a hand.

'Okay, shut up a minute. What ya like at carrying bricks?'

'Carrying bricks, that's my speciality. I'm the bee's knees... the cat's whiskers... the dog's godang......'

'Cut the crap, kid, and follow me.'

The boss led me through the house and out into an overgrown garden. There was a crumbling patio area, numerous trees and bushes and a large disused swimming pool, half filled with stagnant water. Lined along the patio were miscellaneous building materials, sand aggregate, plasterboard - and piles and piles of stacked bricks. While Village People went to get something, I studied the building material and wondered vaguely if I could write a poem about it but there was nothing poetic about the material - it was just a big pile of stuff used to build other stuff.

I jumped onto a pile of bricks and sat there humming a tuneless tune until Village People reappeared. I jumped down and tried to look dynamic. Village People handed me a strange contraption.

'Fuck mate, could only find one of these. You'll be unbalanced but it will have to do.'

The contraption was some sort of portable hand clamp. 'You stick five or six bricks between the vice, grip hard and then off ya go.'

I opened and closed the clamp a few times.

'Take the bricks up to the landing on the fourth floor.'

I glanced at the bricks, there were thousands, a veritable mountain of brick and my spirits plunged to a new low.

'Should be finished by lunch, if ya manage eight at time a?' Said Village People with a chuckle and then disappeared.

I stared at the mountain of bricks. Joseph Ridgwell, the brick poet, I mumbled half-heartedly as I fitted ten bricks into the clamp. Then I gripped tightly and went to walk away but was so unbalanced I fell over.

One of the bricks split in half on impact with the patio. I looked out for any witnesses. There were none, so I disposed of the evidence by kicking the broken brick into some long grass. Luckily I had landed on my good ribs.

The next time around I was more realistic and put only five bricks into the clamp. Then I gripped again and made my way up four flights of stairs.

I spent the entire morning taking brick from the first floor to the fourth, up down, up down, up down, always leaning to one side. During my frequent trips I observed the other builders at work around the house.

They were big, physically strong men, who knew exactly what they were doing. They were at ease in their chosen environment, laughing and cracking jokes, and it made me wonder. How did they do the same shit day after day, year in, year out, without going insane?

At lunch the real builders gave me the cold shoulder and I was left to my own devices. I found a milk bar and bought a ham and cheese sandwich. I walked past a pub that advertised topless go-go and thought about going inside but I didn't.

I found a park and sat on a bench, eating my lunch. I watched some odd-looking birds pecking around and gazed into space. I would have to find easier employment I ruminated as I chewed bread. The life of the poet does not sit comfortably with the life of a labourer, no sir!

The afternoon passed in exactly the same fashion as the morning, except as time went by it became harder and harder to lift bricks from the first to the fourth floor. I tried alternating arms but because of my bad ribs, it didn't make much difference. I took longer and longer breaks between brick lifting and at one point even contemplated jumping out of a fourth floor window and doing away with myself. Then I remembered I hadn't yet produced the great poetry the world needed and fortunately for lovers of ground-breaking verse I decided that, for their sakes, I had to go on living.

At five o'clock, Village People re-appeared just as I was about to carry more brick to the fourth floor.

'Put those down kid, that's enough for one day.'

I didn't need telling twice. Village People pulled a fat wallet from a hip pocket of his shorts - a wallet bulging with cash. I watched as he peeled two fifties from the magnificent wad.

'Here's a days pay. Despite the fact ya don't know ya arse from ya elbow when it comes to power tools an you're a skinny little fucker, I've been pleasantly surprised at your work rate.'

I took the fifties and tried to smile, dead on my feet.

'Cheers boss.'

'Listen. I've got about three or four days' work for ya. Are you okay with that?'

Bollocks, I thought but reckoned three or four days was the most I could manage of this shit before expiring.

'Yeah, no worries, same time tomorrow?'

Village People gave me a friendly slap on the back, which sent me flying.

'Fucking a!'

I left Petersham feeling nothing but fatigue. On the train journey home, I didn't observe the other passengers or think about Rosie but instead struggled to keep my eyes open. At some point, I fell asleep on the shoulder of a smartly dressed woman who politely nudged me away.

At Kings Cross, I fingered the two fifties in my pocket and knew I'd be okay for a few more days. There was also the peanut work to tide me over. Somehow, I would make it.

That night I cooked an improvised dinner on my little one ring hot plate and drunk the last cold beer in the mini-fridge. Then I turned my laptop on and prepared to settle down for an evening of writing but as I waited for the settings to appear, I decided to lie down on the bed. A few hours later, I awoke to the sound of the broken alarm clock beeping. It was time to get up for work.

THIRTEEN.

I toiled at the Petersham building site for the rest of the week and everyday it was the same shit, lifting bricks from the first floor to the fourth floor. On the third day, another labourer appeared to give me a hand. The new guy was an old burnt-out fella in his mid-to-late forties but his age was hard to pinpoint exactly and I never bothered asking for clarification. His name was Trevor. I got on with Trevor straight away. He had no pretensions but boy could he talk. I learned to switch off. He talked mostly about his past life because Trevor was no longer interested in the future. For him it was all about days gone by.

I learned a lot of stuff very quickly. He had been married three times - the first to a childhood sweetheart - a real nice girl who had morphed into a bitch. The second was a bitch from the very beginning and the last, a Filipino girl he'd met in a bar in Manila who, on top of being a bitch, was also a gold-digger. She ran off with his best friend, who was doing well - big house, big car. That Asian bitch wasted no time in getting her claws into him. He no longer spoke to his best friend. Trevor was now single but he had signed up to several dating agencies. He said there were lots of lonely women out there in the world and I believed him.

Trevor once owned several businesses at different times - a window cleaning round, carpet cleaning firm and pizza-delivery outfit. They had all gone bust. Trevor blamed it on his ex-wives and drink but mostly the ex-wives. He liked a beer he said. Trevor's cheeks were permanently red and criss-crossed with broken veins so I reckoned the failures might have had more to do with the drink than he was letting on. He had two grown-up children he never saw. One of the ex's, the mother of his children, had re-located to Fremantle in Western Australia.

'Hell of a long way to visit,' Trevor said without emotion.

We worked hard each day and the mountain of brick shrunk in size until there were more brick on the fourth floor than the first. It was back breaking work and I didn't do any writing. I was tired and didn't go out, not even to look for Rosie. Each evening I came home exhausted, aches and pains all over my body. When one pain disappeared from one locality it was replaced by another pain in another locality. I had to sleep in different positions each night.

Often, as I lay on the bed trying to find a pain free position, I thought about Trevor. He worked just as hard as me but sweated more, moaned more and looked fucked more. All I knew was that I didn't want to be doing the same type of work when I was his age. I'd rather kill myself. Then I wondered how it happened. Did you just wake up one day and find you were old and all the luck gone, or did you wake up one day and find yourself in a big house with a beautiful wife and wondered how you got there?

Then I thought about my life. Where was it headed? Would I ever write any poetry, or was I heading down the same road as old Trevor?

I was consumed by anxieties and fear of an uncertain future and a sneaking suspicion that the world I lived in and what was referred to as society was slowly driving me insane. I didn't get the way people walked, the way they talked, the way they made love, they way they killed each other and other things - their houses, children, schools, offices, governments, rules, laws - I didn't get any of it.

By Friday afternoon, Trevor and I had somehow managed to take every last brick from the first floor to the fourth floor of the building. After the final trip I checked out my arms. They appeared to have stretched a couple of inches longer and in fact, I looked like an orang-utan.

A little while later, Village People showed up for the final pay off. He handed over my last hundred, thanked me for the work and wished me luck. Then he took Trevor round the corner and paid him. I suspected he paid Trevor a little extra but I didn't begrudge this for whatever way I looked at it Trevor needed the money more than me. When Trevor returned, he was thirsty.

'Mate, what d'ya reckon - fancy a schoonie?'

One good thing about working hard all week and not going out was that I now had five hundred dollars burning a hole in my pocket and I was thirsty too.

'Okay.'

I mentioned the pub with the topless go-go and immediately Trevor was up for it and off we went. There was only one girl dancing, an emaciated junkie flinging herself at a lap-dancing pole like she wanted to break her neck. The pub was half-empty. A few men who looked exactly like Trevor sat here and there. Trevor brought the first round, two schooners of New and it wasn't long before he was talking about the past again. I listened patiently - mostly shit about his ex-wives. Well, fuck it. I didn't have anything else to do.

After the fourth schooner, I couldn't bear it any longer. The topless go-go was rubbish and after each crappy dance a scantily-clad junkie appeared and expected you to chuck a dollar or two into a collection tin. Fuck that shit. I decided to head back to the Cross.

Funnily enough, as soon as I mentioned the words, 'The Cross,' Trevor became dewy-eyed. Once more, he re-visited the past - not shit about his wives this time but heady nights in the Cross in the 1980's, when he was a younger man. Suddenly, he wanted to come along, to relive his youth. Okay, I said.

We hit the main drag around seven bells and by now, both of us had acquired a taste for the booze. Trevor was reminiscing all the way, entertaining me with fanciful tales of long forgotten girl-friends, hot chicks, benders, old mates, punch-ups and long since closed bars.

I wasn't listening but Trevor made sure I understood one thing crystal clear. The Cross was no longer the place it had once been and everything had taken a turn for the worse. We walked the main drag and went from bar to bar, drinking steadily, playing pokies and trying to forget all about carrying bricks from the first floor to the fourth.

The night flew by, drinks were drunk, cigarettes were smoked and faces appeared and disappeared. Eventually we found ourselves stuck at the bar of the Goldfish Bowl, chatting to a couple of older sorts, two blondes who were even drunker than we were, muttons dressed as lamb.

I thought about Rosie and told Trevor I was going to the toilet. Trevor had a cigarette stuck in each nostril, one in each ear hole and four or five stuffed in his mouth. The blondes were cracking up. He pulled me aside.

'Hurry back mate - I think we've pulled these two screamers!' he mumbled, two cigarettes shooting out of his mouth as he spoke. I gave him the thumbs up sign and then swerved.

I wandered the main drag. It was early but I was well pissed and having had nothing to eat the fresh air hit me good and strong. I visited all the junkie haunts, hoping to see Rosie but couldn't find her anywhere.

After half an hour of that, I returned to the Goldfish Bowl. When I got there, Trevor and the two blondes had disappeared. I ordered a schooner. Shit, maybe the old fart had lucked out with a threesome. I doubted it but you never can tell.

As I drank the schooner, I remembered the peanut work and the need to get up in the morning. Fuck it. I might as well head back and hit my pit. I sculled the beer and stumbled onto the main drag. I weaved in and out of the crowds of weekend revellers, winding my way towards Roslyn Street and Barncleuth Square.

There were fewer people here. I passed the small square and there she was, Rosie, slumped on a public bench, fast asleep. She looked strung out, head nodding, eyes closed. I sat beside her. She didn't even notice. I sat there for a while and didn't do anything. Then I gently nudged one of her legs.

'Rosie wake up!'

No reaction. I gave her leg a harder nudge.

'Hey Rosie, wake up. It's me, Joseph.'

Her eyes opened sleepily. I saw the blue and felt giddy.

'Mate, what youse doing here?'

'Been drinking with some old codger and working, what you doing?'

Rosie rubbed her hands together very slowly and licked her lips equally as slowly.

'Nothing much, what youse up to?'

I checked the time but was unable to read my watch. I scrunched one eye shut and tried to focus, eventually reducing the many hands to one. It was gone midnight. Hillwood was sure to be asleep by now but with his vampire-like tendencies there was no guarantee.

'D'ya fancy coming back to mine?'

Rosie put a hand on my knee - a simple action that sent an electric current the length of my body, causing all my nerve endings to vibrate and turning me into an electric man.

'Shall we?'

Shall we? Yeah we fucking shall. I grabbed her small hand and led the way.

'Let's boogie baby!'

'Jeez, not that one agin, fella.'

But I didn't care how corny I was. I was with Rosie and that was all that mattered and the night was ours; the world was ours. The only thing that really mattered was that we were together.

At the Oakwoods, we had to tread carefully. If Hillwood woke, that would be the end of everything. I put my keys into the lock like I was threading a needle but I kept missing. Rosie punched me.

'Give me the keys.'

I put a finger to my lips and fell over. I lay on the floor, giggling helplessly. Rosie bent down and grabbed the keys.

'Shit. Hillswood will wake any minute dude!'

Rosie put the key in the lock first time and after tip-toeing past Hillwood's room, suppressing giggles all the way, we made it upstairs without further incident.

Inside my room I went straight to the mini-fridge and opened it, finding it empty.

'Fuck, no booze.'

Rosie pulled something from her jeans.

'Fuck grog, how about something a little ahh… stron-ger?'

I lay down on the bed and tried to keep my eyes open. I was extremely tired. The week of hard work and the booze had got to me. All I wanted to do was sleep.

'Yeah, what's that?'

Rosie unravelled a small wrap of cling film filled with an off brown powder and some tin foil. She spread some powder onto the tin foil. Then she produced a small pipe and lighter. She smoked quickly and with some experience. Then she leaned her head back and stayed that way for a while. When her head returned to its normal position, she smiled at me.

'Wanna get fucked up?'

I'd never taken heroin before but had often been tempted. It was the one drug I was yet to try. Then I remembered a neighbour who had O.D.'d in a flat next to mine, left to decompose in a sweltering Sydney flat for over two weeks before anyone noticed she was dead.

'Okay.'

Rosie handed me the pipe, a MacDonald's straw. Class, I thought, as she heated the drug. Then I inhaled a lung full and sat back.

'I'm fucking ripped, a?' said Rosie.

I couldn't feel anything, apart from my drunkenness but moments later it hit me, an overwhelming wave of nausea. I stood up, wobbled to the sink, and began throwing up. It lasted a while. Rosie comforted me. She helped flush the vomit down the plughole. Eventually I stopped puking.

'Are youse okay?'

I looked in the mirror.

'I've gone green.'

'Green as, a?'

Rosie told me to lie down on the bed, which I did. The room was spinning and I didn't feel good. Fuck heroin, I thought. Rosie chased the dragon a few more times and then lay beside me. I put my arm around her and kissed her on the cheek.

'Do you really like me Joseph?'

I kissed her again, this time on the lips and she poked her tongue into my mouth and wiggled it around. Then I lay my head back on the pillow and closed my eyes.

'Coz I loves ya, I reckon.'

'I oh God...' I muttered before falling into oblivion.

FOURTEEN.

I awoke early. Rosie was still there, lying beside me in the gloomy room - a minor miracle in life. I watched her sleeping and noticed the heroin on the coffee table. There wasn't much left and I wondered what I was letting myself in for. The situation was crazy and there didn't seem anywhere to fit in a happy ending. Why was my life so complicated? Why couldn't I be normal? Then I reminded myself that I was normal and everyone else was insane.

Moments later, the spectre of work reared its revolting head. I checked the clock. Once more, there was no time to lose. I jumped from the bed and dressed. Rosie woke just as I was slipping into my plimsolls.

'Where youse going?' she yawned beautifully.

Her brown breasts, dark nipples and all were showing above the sleeping bag and instantly I wanted to jump her and fuck her madly. After all – crazily - we had yet to make love.

'Work. I'm working at Manly wharf, peanut gig, gotta go now otherwise I'll be late.'

'What am I gonna do?'

'You can stay here - wait for me to get back.'

'When d'ya get back?'

'About half six.'

'I can't stay that long.'

'Okay, stay here for as long as you want, you can let yourself out. Just don't let Hillwood see ya otherwise I'm living on the streets!'

Rosie stood up and walked over, the sleeping bag falling to the floor as she did. I stared at her nakedness. Then she put her arms around me and gave me a great big kiss. Her breath was bad and I was hit by a waft of body odour but even so, it was a beautiful moment.

When she pulled away she looked me direct in the eyes, her eyes incandescent.

'Can't you stay with me?'

'I gotta go,' I said.

I left the Oakwoods at one with the world and despite a raging hangover, feeling futuristic. The sun was shining and it was pleasantly warm. The Sydney skies were dramatically blue, an ocean of azure high above, another great day, in fact.

The ferry ride to Manly was wonderful. I stood on the stern and gazed out to sea. I was so happy I wanted to jump into the harbour and swim with the fishes, touch the seabed, say hello to the dolphins in my mind. It was all too beautiful; all too much to take. I felt a great empathy with the other passengers, old and young. I hoped that everything was good in their life. I smiled, but strangely, they didn't smile back but turned their heads away.

At Manly the day passed quickly. As I now knew the ropes - how to set out the stall, how to caramelise nuts, where to go for lunch - it was straightforward.

The barmaid in the hotel recognised me from the week before and so did a couple of regulars. I played the pokies and lost. Then I plotted up at my observation point. If I had to dash out and serve any customers, the barmaid kept an eye on my schooner. It was always there when I came back.

At the end of the day, the French hippy turned up on time. I hadn't sold much, earning just over fifty dollars but it was money in the pocket. The brick carrying had given me a lifeline; a much-needed breathing space but on Monday I would have to look for a new job.

On the return ferry ride, my thoughts turned to my fledgling relationship with Rosie. I wondered how to make it work. Maybe I could get two jobs, save money and take her away to somewhere safe; somewhere far away from the mean streets of the Cross.

Commuting home on the City rail I wondered if Rosie would still be in my room, sleeping peacefully. At the Oakwoods Hillwood was in his usual spot, squatted on the pavement in front of the apartments and sipping from his disgusting mug.

As I approached, he gave me a funny look and a black cloud of futility positioned itself above my head and remained there hovering ominously. I decided the best tactic was to say nothing, not even hello.

'This is the last time Joseph, no uninvited strangers in the rooms.'

'What? What ya talking about, there was...'

Hillwood ejected a large globule of spit into the gutter, Clint Eastwood style.

'Especially street kids. Security risk, theft issues.'

Fucking hell! This was the second time the old goat had insulted my one true love. I bit my lip, said nothing and walked away.

'Last chance.'

Fuck you Hillwood, fuck you very much! I jumped the stairs and up to my room, but on opening the door I found it empty. I collapsed onto the bed fully clothed, knackered, beat but content. The presence of Rosie permeated the fetid atmosphere of the enclosed walls, a stale, rancid, sour odour but just how heaven would smell, I reasoned.

I closed my eyes and imagined Rosie naked with me on top. When that was over, I found an old tee-shirt and wiped off. It was then and only then that I noticed it missing. The laptop!

I turned the room upside down. Still no laptop. There could be only one culprit. Rosie. I paced the room in tiny circles, cursing the love of my life. I couldn't believe she'd done it. My fucking laptop! The only material possession I couldn't afford to lose. How would I write any poetry without it?

How? What d'ya mean how? Paper and pens you mug! Computers are a recent invention; think of all the others that have gone before you. Did Homer use a laptop to compose the Odyssey? And what about Virgil, Keats, Bryon, Li Po – what did they use to compose their masterpieces? For thousand of years man has been content with pens and paper. Fuck it. Some of those greats didn't even have pens, they used chalk, slate, quills!

I found some paper and a pencil. I was in a fury; a man possessed. I quickly jotted down three Odes, one after the other: Bitch I, Bitch II and Bitch III - the words pouring from me - disgusting adjectives, fiery metaphors and accusing similes.

I struck a defiant pose and read the poems aloud, whilst glancing in the mirror. The poems were terrible; filled with bitterness and bile, nothing poetic, no beauty. I tore the papers into a thousand pieces and threw them out of the window, watching as they fluttered earthwards like a one-man ticker tape parade.

After that, I rushed to the nearest bottle shop and brought a 2- litre cask of rotgut vino. I didn't even look for Rosie along the main drag. Waste of time. She would have fucked off to some other junkie haunt to sniff the proceeds from the sale of my laptop up her nose. Fuck her. I hope the crazy bitch OD's, I thought, evilly. Then I returned to my room, filled a dirty glass with cheap plonk and drank until passing out.

FIFTEEN.

The next day I awoke to find my tiny bed-sit glowing like the inside of a cathedral or an expectant mother's womb. Sunlight streamed through a multitude of gaps in the softly flapping, tattered curtain and it was hot. I saw the cask of rotgut wine, grabbed it and took a hit; remarkably, it was half full. The vino still tasted like horseshit but immediately afterwards I felt better. Then I remembered the laptop. I glanced to where it had once been; a square outline of dust the only indicator of its presence.

After cursing Rosie several times, I tore the ragged curtain aside and peered outside. The Sunday morning streets were deserted and for most ordinary folk, the weekend was already over but not for me. I wasn't about to let my sacred Sunday be affected by any oppressive thoughts of Monday mornings at work. Hey, who cares about any of it? Okay Rosie, had robbed me blind but what did I care? It was Sunday. The sun was shining and the allure of the beach was all around. I found a crumpled cigarette, lit it, blew out a cloud of smoke and felt immortal.

Half a litre of rotgut vino later, I caught the 324 bus and headed to Watson's bay in a boozy frame of mind. I jumped off the bus just before Rose Bay and the school of the Sacred Heart and headed to a little-known series of tiny coves and bays dotted along the edges of Sydney harbour. I could've gone to one of the popular surf beaches, Bondi, Manly, Coogie, or Bronte but they would've been oversubscribed with people and surfers and I hated surfers, or at least the modern day equivalent of a surfer. Snobbish, elitist and fascist in their ways, they had little time for the casual swimmer or for anyone who wasn't stuck to a stunted piece of fibreglass coated foam. Dullards!

Anyway, I needed solitude and respite from everything. There were a few sheltered beaches near Rose Bay where a body could be alone, where a troubled man could find some serenity and re-focus. I couldn't wait to jump into the cool water. Natural hydrotherapy - that's what I needed.

Once on the coastal path, I gazed at the horizon. The city of Sydney was laid out before me like a cardboard cut-out, shimmering in the haze of summer's first onslaught. I was the only one on the path. I didn't have a clue where the fuck the other four million Sydneysiders were but I was glad they were elsewhere. Slung over my shoulder was a cheap cooler-bag purchased from Crazy Prices, inside which resided a six-pack of Toohey's Red.

I joined the path just as it wound its dusty way along the bottom of a nun's cemetery. The school of the Sacred Heart had once been a convent and here, in front of the deep blue sea was the resting place of many of that religious order.

I looked at the crosses and read some of the names; Sister this, Sister that - all long dead and gone forever. It was hot now. I pulled out a bottle of sparkling ale, chilled to perfection, took a hit and thought about those dead nuns and wondered if they had all died virgins. What a waste of pussy.

I took in deep breaths of sea air and unlike the dead nuns, felt alive. In this mood, Rosie was forgiven and welcomed back into my affections with open arms. How could I let a cheap piece of machinery get in the way of a brand new love affair? For after all, she loved me - her words, from her mouth!

Pretty soon, I came to the beach I was looking for; a small strip of sand, overshadowed by series of sandstone rocks. I put my cooler bag down and sat under the shade of a fig tree strewn with jungle-like vines. There was no one else around. Towering high above me were the mansions of Vaucluse, one of Sydney's most desirable and expensive residential areas and here was me, the aspiring poet, enjoying the little beach for free.

I looked at those mansions for signs of life but there were none, just big empty soulless houses, with nothing going on, ever. Well fuck them and their money. It was better to be alive, to feel free, if only for a moment in time.

After downing a couple of beers I decided to go for a swim. I stripped naked and run into the sea, diving into the water with the elegance of a seal. Ah, it was great to feel the water caress my nakedness, so I swum and swum.

I floated on my back. In the distance, fishing boats, sailing yachts and motor boats bobbed along and the surface of the water looked like someone had chucked a million diamonds across its surface. This is what it's all about, I thought, as I began a slow underwater wank; concentrating on an image of Rosie naked and afterwards, watching contentedly as the spermatozoa floated to the bottom of the deep blue sea.

I experienced a little panic after that. I'd read somewhere that dolphins have vaginas remarkably similar to that of a human. I wondered what would happen if my spunk somehow slipped into a female dolphin? I mean - would it be possible for it to give birth to a mermaid or merman?

Just as I was about to emerge from the water, a family appeared on the scene and plotted up a few metres from the vine-strewn fig tree and my stuff. This freaked me out and disturbed my isolated beach equilibrium.

There were four adults and seven kids, so it wasn't even your bog standard nuclear family but an extended motherfucker. I gnashed my teeth and shook my fist at them, when they weren't looking. I wondered how I was going to leave the sea without one of them getting a front row view of my crown jewels. I floated on my back some more and contemplated this tricky predicament philosophically.

Eventually I grew cold and thirsty. The skin on my hands and feet began to shrivel up until I resembled a human prune. Fuck it. The family of interlopers - on what I considered to be my own private beach - would have to cop a view of my cock and balls swinging free. I left the water. I didn't run but took my time, figuring if they were going to see my nakedness they might as well get a good look. They all got a good look. After a leisurely stroll across the sand I reached my towel and covered up.

Moments later, a female from the extended family approached. I was sucking on my fourth Toohey's Red and feeling groovy.

'Excuse me,' said she.

'Yo,' I replied languidly.

'This is not a nudist beach. There are several designated nudist beaches and this isn't one of them. What you just did was a breach of…and I have a young…..'

Blah, blah, blah. The woman was talking but I wasn't listening, total waffle. I registered moving lips and noted how every now and again she made gestures with her hands but fuck her and the rules. I mean what the fuck was I supposed to do?

I took another swig of beer and entertained thoughts of putting an ice pick straight through her annoying head. Then I heard myself apologising, saying the beach was empty when I'd arrived and there wasn't anyone around etc. The subjugation of my own voice disgusted me. Why didn't I just tell the stupid bitch to fuck off and die?

I remained on the beach for a while afterward but whatever satisfaction I'd enjoyed before was gone forever. When I left, the family were in the middle of a game of beach cricket. Needless to say, I didn't say goodbye.

I decided to walk all the way back to the Cross. It was a long walk but a pleasant one and on the way I stopped off at several bottle shops and brought longnecks for the journey.

By the time I reached the outskirts of the Cross I was drunk but as I stumbled along Elizabeth Bay Road I saw it; the sign. I stopped dead in my drunken tracks and read the sign several times. Then I stepped back and assessed the building. It was a care home for the elderly or some form of sheltered accommodation. There was a name attached to the brickwork in big white letters.

CAMELOT APARTMENTS.

SIXTEEN.

I peeked inside. Several old people were sat in a small coffee shop talking and drinking. There was two staff in the café; a middle -aged white man and an old Filipino woman. The man was talking to the old people and laughing, while the Filipino washed dishes. I read the sign one more time.

Help Wanted
Porter Required
Nights
Good rates of Pay

Fucking hell, this sounded like my ideal job. Do fuck all during the night, read a bit, sneak a few catnaps and spend the day-times writing poetry. I'd done similar work before and there was a good chance of landing the job if I applied. I checked my reflection in a car window. I was visibly drunk. There was no way I could apply for the job in such a state. I cursed my drunken ways. If sober, I could've applied for the job there and then. Fuck it. I would have to cross my fingers, hoped no one applied for the job in the interim and return first thing in the morning.

The next day, despite the prospect of a steady earner, I woke late and it was mid-morning by the time I rolled up to the Camelot Apartments.

I was nervous, waves of anxiety verging on panic, washed over me with each step. My palms were sweaty and I was shaky.

Then I saw the sign still there, in the window. I paced the pavement and composed myself. Why was I so jumpy? It was only a night porter's gig for fucksakes! I reckoned my excessive consumption of booze was making me jittery and vowed to taper off my drinking and get straight.

I opened the door and walked into the coffee shop with what I supposed were purposeful strides. The friendly middle-aged man was there and the Filipino woman, occupying identical positions to the day before.

A couple of old biddies sat in one corner looking half- dead. Despite overpowering fragrances of roses, lemon and lime and other air-fresheners wafting around, the smell of old people dying permeated the atmosphere. I took a few sniffs. I liked it - the smell of death.

'How can I help?' asked the man.

I checked out that voice and immediately my gaydar switched on. A fading queen but not in any way camp, which was a good sign. I've got nothing against homosexuals but the overtly camp ones bore me; all those endless sexual innuendos and histrionics masking an otherwise embittered and twisted freak.

'Erm, I've come about the Night Porter vacancy.'

The man introduced himself as Stuart and then led me into a little office. I needn't have fretted so much beforehand because landing the job was a piece of piss. Stuart asked a few obligatory questions; previous experience, visa status etc. I showed him my old tax file number and mumbled something about a misplaced passport but fortunately Stuart wasn't concerned with bureaucracy - he just needed to fill the position.

The job was Thursday to Sunday, eight-hours a day, ten through to six - thee old graveyard shift. I put my autograph on a contract of employment and the job was mine on a casual basis. Could I start this Thursday? Yes, I replied, knowing the best part of three days of freedom lay ahead of me; a breathing space. Stuart issued another of his warm smiles and we shook hands.

Afterwards Stuart gave me a brief guided tour of the complex. Despite being populated with coffin dodgers, the Camelot was a snazzy place, six floors of one, two and three-bedroom apartments. It had a roof-terrace with harbour views, lounge room, restaurant and a hair salon.

In my mind's eye, I compared the joint to the Oakwoods and would've swapped places at the drop of a hat. Despite being on the cusp of non-existence, those old codgers were obviously rich old codgers and wanted for nothing.

There was a twenty-four hour paging system. My job was to man reception and deal with room service requests. Whatever way I looked at it, it appeared to be a cushy number. Those pensioners were bound to spark out early each evening and I figured I'd be able to write at work. Hey, hey! Happy days for an aspiring poet.

Just as I was about to leave, Stuart pulled me aside and asked if I'd ever done any waiting.

'Yes,' I lied.

Would I like to wait at a wedding of a friend of his this Wednesday? Hmm, my last days of freedom were now whittled down to two but of course I would. $150 for around four or five hours work - mostly just topping up wine glasses. Fucking hell. My ship had come in.

Stuart gave me an address. It was an evening service and reception. I thought this strange but said nothing. What the fuck did I care? Day or night, it was still $150 smackeroonies.

Then Stuart gave me the once over. Did I have any smart clothes? White shirt, dark tie, black trousers? Fuck it. I had none of that shit. I shook my head sadly and said sayonara to those one hundred and fifty big ones. Stuart shot me another of those warm smiles of his. Don't worry he said, he knew of someone who could help. He led me outside and pointed to a small garage some way along the street.

'Go over there and speak to Bill. Tell him Stuart sent you and tell him the occasion and what you need. He manages a second hand clothes stall for a local charity; he'll have something for you.'

I walked away feeling glad in my heart. Unwarranted kindness from a complete stranger was a rare occurrence but maybe the big fella upstairs had spotted Rosie stealing my laptop and decided it was payback time. I walked along, marvelling at the wonder of life in all its ugliness and beauty.

At the garage, another fading queen confronted me. He was an otherwise ordinary looking man in his mid to late fifties but the pink fluorescent socks were the giveaway. I fed him the line from Stuart and he morphed into charm personified. Come this way, he urged as he stood amidst rows and rows of old clothes.

The aged fairy led me to an improvised changing room at the back of the garage. It was dark back there but there was a full-length mirror. Pink socks rifled through rows of shirts and trousers.

'Now, has Stuart told you anything about who is getting married?'

'Na.'

'He hasn't? Oh well, it'll make for a nice surprise. Now get undressed, while I find an appropriate outfit. Some of Sydney's finest will be attending this wedding, so we'll have you looking spick and span.'

I didn't have a clue what the old fart was talking about but as a favour was being bestowed on yours truly, I obeyed like a docile minion. Luckily I hadn't gone commando like usual.

As I stood there in my boxers, keeping my eyes peeled for any funnel-web spiders, Bill rushed around the cramped interior of the garage, tossing articles over his shoulders and arms.

When he cried out for measurements, I replied I wasn't sure what mine were. He stopped what he was doing, grinned manically and produced a tape measure. Then he measured me up, rubbing his hands along my naked waist and down my hairy legs with disconcerting enthusiasm. Randy old goat!

When that was over Bill began handing me items of clothing in rapid succession, six pairs of trousers, several shirts, three pairs of black shoes and a plethora of ties. The garage was situated in the middle of one of Sydney's more affluent suburbs and most of it was decent clobber - designer names, quality material. I felt almost rich. To me all the clothes looked good but Bill disagreed and got me to try on article after article, noting that nothing looked quite right each time.

Every time I revealed some nakedness Bill appeared visibly excited, so for a laugh I decided to accidentally pull my boxers down and give old Billy boy a front row view of my youthful bum cheeks.

After trying on another pair of decent trousers that didn't quite fit Bills exacting requirements, I whipped them and my boxers off simultaneously.

'Oops,' I said.

I thought Bill was going to have a heart attack, beads of sweat popped out all over his forehead and his cheeks turned as red as a beet. Easy tiger! I bagged a smart pair of black trousers, a pair of leather brogues, one spotless white cotton shirt and a purple Italian silk tie.

'Erm, ow much is all this gonna set me back?' I said, hoping that the free view of my youthful derriere had merited a freebie. And I was right, for as soon as payment was mentioned Bill waved his hands in the air.

'For you, dear boy, nothing at all. Consider it a gift from the charitable trust and a favour to my good friend Stuart.'

I said nothing but gave the big fella upstairs an imaginary salute.

'And remember to enjoy the night. I'm sure you will never have experienced anything like it before,' Bill added, mysteriously.

I hurried back to the Oakwoods to try on my new clothes and pretend I was a big shot western playboy with a yacht moored in the Ernest Hemingway marina, Havana.

SEVENTEEN

The next day was Tuesday. My last day of freedom! As it was hot I went for a swim in the pool and swum three hundred mini-lengths. After that exertion, I enjoyed a leisurely hour in the Jacuzzi. Then I retreated to my room.

In the evening, I received a message from the French hippy peanut man, via Hillwood, the decrepit one delivering the news personally. Apparently, I'd been fired for drinking on duty.

I thanked Hillwood for the information and told him that it saved me the trouble of resigning. Then, with a big smile, I told him about the other job. Hillwood was unable to hide his disappointment and sloped off without another word.

That night I remained sober. I sat in my room and tried to write some poetry with paper and pen but sober or drunk it was the same result, total nothingness. After a couple of hours I gave up.

Then I saw my new/second hand clothes, slipped into them, and admired myself in the mirror. I looked good; sharp as a pencil and knew I was meant for better things. I deserved the finest clothes, hotels, cars and restaurants. They were my divine right!

As these thoughts harangued my brain, a sound I recognised immediately pierced the air.

'Psst, Psst!'

I peered out of my window and there she was, leaning against the same palm tree. Rosie! Waving and flashing her trademark dopey smile. On the way down to meet her I was excited and nervous, they way I always felt on seeing her. I kept my eyes peeled for Hillwood but fortunately his door was firmly shut.

I signalled for Rosie to come over and after hesitating, she did, albeit tentatively. Then we crept up the stairs together and stood outside my room. Rosie looked me up and down, surprised by the getup I was in.

'Where's the funeral bro?'

I grabbed her arm.

'Shut up,' I snapped.

I slammed the door of my room shut and stood in front of it, barring any means of escape. Rosie collapsed onto the bed. She didn't look so good. She had changed - grown thinner and sported the remnants of a tasty black eye. Her appearance shocked me but I wanted answers.

'Right, first things first. Who gave ya the shiner?'

Rosie looked at me sadly, her eyes welling up, 'Three wogs in Parramatta, they beat us over a $20 rock. One of tha' bastards punched us and called us a petrol-sniffing nigger bitch!'

'They what? Those greasy scummed-out fucks!'

I felt a devastating surge of anger directed to all the disgusting and horrible men in the world, which was easily over 90% of the male population - all a bunch of misogynist cowardly prick fucks. Why would someone do that, to someone as vulnerable and helpless as my Rosie?

'Parramatta? What the fuck were you doing over there?'

'I go there nows and then. Sometimes good business an I's got good connections.'

When it came down to it I knew hardly anything about this mystery girl, who she really was and how she lived her life. Nothing but love is blind and I could see nothing and everything. Then I remembered the laptop.

'And why the...' but before I got any further Rosie jumped from the bed, threw her arms around me and burst into tears.

'What's wrong?'

'Do youse hate me Joseph?'

Did I hate her, no of course not. I just didn't like being taken for a mug. After several unnaturally tight bear hugs I pushed her away and looked into her sad blue eyes.

'Why did you take it?'

Rosie wiped her nose and sobbed once more. 'I don't know, I needed the monies. He said he was gonna kill me if I didn't produce.'

'Who?'

'My dealer a? I owed monies.'

This was something else to consider, drug debts.

'Why didn't ya tell me?'

Rosie fell onto the bed again.

'I wanted to tell ya Joseph but I thought ya wouldn't help me. I mean, why should youse help me?'

Instinctively, I knew I would help this girl until the end of time or at least until I couldn't take being mugged off anymore.

'Look Rosie, don't you understand. You said you loved me and then ya stole my laptop, how do I work that one out?'

'I think I do love ya Joseph but why d'ya love me? Everyone says youse got a screw loose.'

Another surge of anger, this time towards all the fucking judgemental people in the world, which again was a fair few billion mother-freaks.

'Fuck everyone. How the fuck do they know how I feel? Who the fuck are they to me?'

'Oh, Joseph!'

I put my arms around Rosie and kissed her. She responded and we kissed for ages, our tongues exploring each others mouths like mad probes. After the snake-like kiss we lay together on the bed.

'So how much did you get for it?'

'Wha?'

'The laptop.'

'One fifty.'

'One fifty? It's worth three times that at least!'

'Yeah, that's what I thought but those pricks in Happy Hockers are tight a – really fucking tight!'

'How much to get it out of hock?'

'One fifty plus interest.'

'What are the interest rates?'

Rosie shrugged her shoulders.

'Fuck it. They can keep it. From now on, I go traditional.'

'What?'

'Sorry. I mean I'm gonna do all my writing in longhand. Fuck technology, I'm disconnecting from all that electronic inhumane shit!'

'Ah, shit. I forgot youse is a poet.'

'The world's greatest!'

'Ya sure pom?'

'Incontestable fact, which calls for a celebration. Booze?'

'I guess so, yeahs, why not a?'

I nipped out and purchased a slab of Toohey's Red and a half pint of vodka so we could get good and boozy. We sat in my room, drinking and talking. We talked for ages, then we kissed for ages and then we were naked, lying together in that cramped room; two young people with nowhere to go but down.

'Let's root,' whispered Rosie into my ear, her words coated in layers of lust and booze. I got on top and looked at Rosie; the small brown body, pert breasts, brown nipples, dark pubic hair and knew it was now or never. I manoeuvred into position but all the while thinking about the life she was leading, the people she was involved with. Well, fuck them and fuck everything. I slid in and gasped at the feeling. I heard Rosie groan and let myself go; lost myself in passion. Drunk, the words of love came easy and Rosie cried and clawed my back, wrapping her skinny legs around my torso, like a human clam. And then, just before I unloaded, Rosie cried and grabbed my balls, squeezing tight.

There was no way I could hold out any longer - not that I wanted to - and I pumped days, weeks and months worth of frustration into her, collapsing, exhausted, drowned in a sea of passion.

We seemed to make an even deeper connection after that and talked late into the night. With the booze flowing freely, we made rudimentary plans to get out of the Cross and do something with our lives. I told Rosie about my job as a porter. I could save up, buy a cheap car and we could drive across the country; move to another city. Had she ever been to Brisbane? No she hadn't. Good - we'd go there!

Rosie was excited by all the big talk. She hadn't really been anywhere and I talked a good game. It would be possible for us to live together, rent a flat, get steady jobs, quit the drugs, get away from the streets, and lead a normal life like everyone else. Rosie fell for it, her blue eyes sparking with all the possibilities being fed to her, by me, Joseph Ridgwell: the world's greatest liar.

EIGHTEEN.

We spent the most of the next day shagging until we just couldn't shag anymore. After the eighth shag my dick gave up the ghost and Rosie became convinced she would never be able to walk again. My wedding gig wasn't until 7pm, so I relished the chance to laze in bed for a few hours.

The sex had been fantastic, but gruelling, the extended session leaving me exhausted, and with a lingering feeling of emptiness. Rosie had been more or less insatiable - never refusing my advances and always ready for more. Despite her sideline on the streets, we hadn't used a condom and neither of us mentioned anything about protection. The night before, I hadn't given it a moment's thought, I'd just stuck it in and enjoyed it but now, in the harsh, dusty, yellow light of early morn, fearful regrets infiltrated my brain.

As far as I knew, this girl was fucking any man that had a few dollars in his pocket; builders, street cleaners, gangsters, junkies, pimps, ponces, perverts - anyone. A wave of anxiety hit me hard, what about my health? What about STD's and HIV?

I grilled Rosie about her use of protection, grasping for some form of reassurance. She always used condoms and was on the pill. She also had regular check-ups and tests. She was clean, she said but I wasn't convinced and the fears remained. But what could I do? The act had been committed and there was no turning back. I'd never taken an AIDS test in my life, so who was I to judge?

After the first couple of morning roots, Rosie started in on the beers again and it wasn't long before I joined her. She might have been five years younger but when it came to getting wasted she was pure hardcore. And she didn't discriminate.

During our conversations I discovered she'd taken everything - cannabis, LSD, speed, heroin, cocaine and a whole host of non-prescribed prescription drugs - anything that would get her high in fact. And on top of all this she drank like a fish. The only thing she didn't do was needles.

'Promise me you won't ever start injecting that shit.'

Rosie took a swig of her beer.

'Don't worry, I hate needles. They scare tha fuck outta me.'

I wasn't convinced. It was only a matter of time. In the right place, with the right people, she'd start shooting up. But as I'd taken the same drugs I wasn't in a position to give a lecture. Anyway, I didn't have anything against heroin, alcohol was just as bad but because of its illegality, smack was like playing Russian roulette and once addicted, you were in it for the long run. After my third beer, I decided to stop drinking.

'This is gonna be my last beer,' I told Rosie, 'don't wanna show up for work stinking of booze.'

With that announcement Rosie appeared deflated, like what I'd said had used up all the energy in the room. She was silent for a few moments.

'What's up?' I asked.

'What if I pop out and get a little powder?'

'Smack?'

'Yeah, just a 20 bag, to chill with.'

For some perverse reason, the idea appealed to my sensibilities – anyway, smoking it was harmless wasn't it? I pulled a lobster from my pocket.

'Okay but as soon as we get out of the Cross we cut all this shit out. Agreed?'

'Even the grog?'

'Let's not get carried away - just all Class A's.'

Once I'd checked the coast was clear, Rosie went on the mission. She was gone for over an hour. I lay on my bed thinking she wasn't coming back but I wasn't annoyed - maybe I was getting used to it. Then I heard it again; the psst, psst sound. Once safely inside my room Rosie got out the bag, tin foil and MacDonald's straw. She heated the drug and smoked quickly, just like a pro.

'I won't get sick again will I?'

Rosie laughed at my inexperience; she the old hand at nineteen, me five years older and totally green. Then I smoked some and this time round I managed to smoke it myself, chasing thee old dragon as it swirled into the atmosphere.

For the first ten minutes, I felt nothing and kept asking Rosie why nothing was happening. She told me to shut up and wait a while. Then it hit; almost imperceptibly at first but gradually pleasant sensations unleashed themselves inside my body, riding my spine and pounding the base of my skull. Rosie was laughing at me but I didn't care; in fact I didn't care about anything because nothing mattered. Writing was ridiculous; poetry absurd, the patrons of such arts demented and the artists themselves a bunch of pretentious, preening egotists. Even wog boys raping and beating my girl in Parramatta became a minor trifle in life. What mattered was that I felt good and Rosie stayed by my side, the rest of the world could fuck off and die.

Rosie leaned over and kissed me.

'Good shit, a?'

'Fucked.'

'I fucking loves it Joseph.'

I rolled my eyes and licked my lips.

'I fucking love you.'

Rosie nestled her head against my neck.

'I fucking love you too.'

This sequence of profanity made us laugh a slow, languid junkie laugh, which despite our happiness, echoed hollow and transient.

NINETEEN.

We left the Oakwoods at five, me to my wedding gig in Paddington and Rosie off to visit friends in Woolloomooloo. Unfortunately, we timed our exit dead wrong because waiting outside, in his usual position, was Hillwood. There was nothing we could do except walk straight past. I prepared myself for a lecture, a threat of eviction but surprisingly the old goat said nothing, not even hello.

'Funny,' I remarked afterwards.

'Weird shit,' said Rosie.

Before splitting, we arranged to meet on Sunday and go to the beach. I'd told Rosie all about the little secluded cove near Rose Bay. Although born and bred in Sydney, she'd never been anywhere near Rose Bay, or any beaches for that matter, not even Bondi. We arranged to meet outside Mansions Hotel at ten o'clock. I made Rosie promise to be there by crossing her heart and hoping to die. Then I watched her walk away until she disappeared around a corner.

On the way to Paddington I was chilled but also listless. The heroin buzz had long since dissipated and the after-effects had left me in a zombiefied state. Despite this, the directions given to me by Stuart were easy to follow and I found the location at the first attempt.

As soon as I got to the location, however, something was amiss. For one thing, some architectural features of the Church were distinctly odd.

Sticking out of the large wooden door of the entrance were two great sword handles, which was unusual and there was none of the usual church paraphernalia - service times, fluorescent messages -from- Jesus posters. Most of the windows were blacked out but out front was a catering van and lots of people coming and going. There was a sign saying, 'Wedding This Way,' beneath which was an arrow pointing to the entrance of the church. I was to ask for a man called Daniel.

Daniel was another fag, so no surprise there but he was a lot younger than Bill or Stuart, with perfect tan, perfect physique and perfect hair. The male model took me inside the alleged church and gave me the low down. I was to start uncorking bottles of wine and fill glasses. When the guests arrived, I was to walk around topping up their glasses. Then Daniel fired a warning at me: at no time was a guest to be left standing with an empty glass, this could not be allowed to happen. Got it?

I got it all right but although I paid attention to what old Danny boy was telling me, the interior of the church was a distraction and it was hard not to look around in wonder. After a few more instructions on what to do, male model Daniel handed me a waiter's friend and told me to get to work on the bottles.

I studied the interior of the building whilst uncorking bottles. The only traditional church items were a black font and pulpit surrounded by purple and gold velvet drapes. In place of pews and altar, was a large stage and wooden dance floor but most impressive was a mural running the entire length of one wall. It depicted the seven deadly sins in terrifying Goya like images; Lust, Gluttony, Greed, Sloth, Wrath, Envy and Pride staring down at me.

If anything, the church looked like the inside of a fabulous gothic nightclub. I walked over to several tables that were positioned end-to-end and covered in black cloth. Behind the table were rows of stacked cardboard boxes. I opened the boxes and took out glasses and bottles of red wine. As I worked, some more male models appeared carrying several coffin-like polystyrene boxes. They filled the boxes with ice and placed bottles of white wine and beers inside.

There were four of us behind the table - all definitely gay - except little old me and I began to wonder about this here wedding.

'Strange church,' I said to the fag beside me.

'This is a Satanist church,' said the guy.

'Oh.'

'Yes, in here they worship Lucifer, Satan and the fallen angels. They believe you create your own destiny.'

'Freaky.'

So that explained the seven deadly sins mural, I thought but there was no homage to the evil one in evidence; the old devil himself. Still, I liked the sound of creating your own destiny.

I continued un-corking bottles and filling glasses while people rushed around. Presents arrived by the box load - expensive looking presents - in lavish packaging. The stage began to transform. Lights were set up, some dancers practiced dance routines, a DJ appeared, huge speakers and lighting equipment were rolled in. Instead of a wedding reception it looked like the preparations for a boy band disco.

The gays worked faster than me and were more adept at uncorking the bottles with their waiter's friend. I wasn't sure if it was the heroin and four-day hangover combo but my movements were sluggish and uncoordinated. And I was clumsy. I smashed a glass and spilled some wine on the floor. This annoyed the gays and they quickly lost patience with me. This was followed by a series of bitchy comments made to each other.

Feeling freaky, I decided I needed a drink and when the gays weren't looking I took sly swigs from the bottles. After a few swigs I was revitalised and my work rate improved. The gays appreciated my improvement.

'So who's getting married?' I asked.

'Don't you know?'

'Na.'

'Tonight is one of the biggest events of the season, to celebrate the union of Mitch Dowd and Trent Nathan. Anyone who's anyone on the scene will be here. You should feel privileged.'

I smiled and said I felt very privileged, a lie which pleased the gay no end but suddenly everything made sense. Names such as Mitch and Trent and all-gay staff could only mean one thing. I was about to attend my very first fairy wedding, well fuck a duck!

Pretty soon everything was set for the gig/disco/wedding and then guests began to arrive. By this time I'd swigged a whole bottle of red and was feeling boozy and more than looking forward to experiencing another life first.

I observed the guests meandering around the hall like lost children in a department store. There were far more men than women but everyone male and female were dressed to kill and oozed success and money. I'd never seen so many handsome men in one place. They all looked like film stars or football players but there was something wrong with them. They were too perfect, almost unnatural looking, like they'd never been tested.

According to my new co-workers this collection of beautiful people was Sydney's glitterati and they gave me a running commentary. Who was who; who was the richest, who was the most famous, who was almost famous, who used to be famous, who thought they were famous etc. But along with the running commentary, came the gossip and bitchiness -'Look at how that is dressed, look at the state of her (him), who does she think she is? (Another him). Fuck me; it was like working with a bunch of old women.

Soon, the main event was underway. There were representatives from each family - mums, dads, sisters, brothers and a dazzling lightshow - lasers, strobes and dry ice. Instead of Wagner's Bridal Chorus or Mendelssohn's wedding march, the homos opted to lead with the Ronette's classic Be My Baby and exited with Dusty Springfield's jaunty Stay Awhile. I was impressed - both tunes sounding far groovier than the traditional dirges.

Everything was topsy-turvy. The Mother gave away the groom. The priest was a Drag Queen. The best man was a woman. The pageboys and bridesmaids were professional dancers, who broke out into well-choreographed dance moves as soon as music blasted from the speakers.

Once the rings were swapped and vows exchanged, the disco started. I was ordered to circulate among the guests with tray after tray of wine glasses. Then, with a tea towel draped over one arm, I was ordered to circulate and top up any half-filled glasses. I was shown how to do this correctly by holding the bottom of the wine bottle and turning clockwise. I weaved in and out of the guests, topping up glasses and every now and then having a secret swig for myself. In this way, the night flew by.

The disco was loud and raucous. There was a couple of lively drag shows and even some jugglers and fire-eaters. The dance floor was crowded. People were drunk and high and letting themselves go. My job gradually became less and less hectic, until eventually I just handed drinks to people as and when they approached the tables. It was a piece of piss. At some point one of the gays even told me to help myself to a beer, which I did and gladly.

Around eleven, the lights went up and the guests were instructed to move on to a party being held on some yachts in Darling harbour. Funnily enough, everyone appeared to be invited to the yacht bash except me, not that I cared. I was half- cut already and just wanted to get my $150 and fuck off to prepare myself for my first day of work at the Camelot Apartments.

Around midnight, the clean up operation was complete and all I had to do was wait around for my pay. All my co-workers were heading to the party on the boat and I felt like a bit of a plank, sitting there, uninvited and straight.

Finally, the Head Gay appeared and began handing out cash. As he did, he gave each of the other gays a kiss full on the lips but when it came to me he just handed the notes over and shook my hand. I walked away with mixed emotions.

TWENTY.

I spent the whole of the next day in bed, farting continuously and hung over. The beer fart hours passed quickly and I drifted in and out of sleep in a hazy dreamtime fashion.

Mad visions entertained my sub-conscious; visions of Rosie, visions of perfect homosexuals, visions of immortality, visions of Rosie with other men and finally visions of my own death. Several times, I awoke in a cold sweat, shaking with fear; my heart pounding and my sleeping-bag soaked through.

At five, I finally roused from my self-imposed lethargy and decided to go for a swim in the Oakwoods pool. It was then that I saw the note. I read it with worried eyes. It was from Hillwood. Apparently, he wanted to speak to me about an 'urgent' matter. I screwed the note into a ball and lobbed it over my shoulder. Fuck him, I thought. Then I went for a swim.

The pool was empty and the garden deserted, with most of the residents at work. I jumped into the pool and swum a few half-hearted lengths, floated on my back and did some underwater handstands. Then I jumped into the Jacuzzi. It was switched off but warmer than the pool itself. I lay there and stared at the sky. The sky was blue.

---

[1] This saying is not found in the Koran or the Canonical Traditions, and may have been "made up" by mystics or even heretics.

One of the methadone lesbians appeared. The fat one, munching from a bowl of Sugar Puffs, ladling spoonfuls of cereal into her cavernous mouth. I said hi and resumed sky gazing.

'Hillwood's looking for you, Pom,' she said between mouthfuls.

'Is he around?'

'In his room.'

I thought about the note. It was certain the 'urgent matter' had something to do with Rosie and asking me to leave. I jumped out of the pool and wrapped a towel around my waist. Fuck it. Might as well find out what the old goat wants. I would just tell him that Rosie was my girlfriend, who, in fact, she was and there were no rules against bringing partners to the rooms. How could there be? That would be an infringement of basic human rights.

I squelched into the hallway and rapped loudly on Hillwood's door, dripping chlorinated water everywhere. No decrepit landlord was going to intimidate me I thought angrily; I was no ordinary schmuck. I'd grown up on a council estate in London's notorious East End and knew how to handle myself.

The sound of many locks rattling commenced. After an age half of the door opened, just like the doors in stables do, but instead of a horse's head the ugly mug of Hillwood appeared. I stepped back in surprise. I'd never noticed this feature before and for a split second it threw me.

'Ah, it's you,' said Hillwood.

'You wanted to see me, about an urgent matter.'

With that Hillwood reeled out the same old lines. No uninvited guests allowed in the rooms. Safety issues, security issues, especially with the company I was keeping. When I told him Rosie was my girlfriend, he laughed. Girls like that don't have boyfriends, he said with a sneer; only mugs. I contemplated upping the old fart, sticking two fingers in his eyeballs, or a flying head butt to the nose.

'Listen kid. I'm only trying to do you a favour.'

'How d'ya work that out?'

'She's a black fella and with black fellas the best policy is to steer well clear.'

This outrageous and unexpected comment stunned me into silence.

'You're a good looking kid, why d'ya wanna hang around with lowlife like that? All she'll do is steal from ya and then drag you into the gutter!'

At the mention of the word 'steal' I blushed bright red. Hillwood clocked my discomfort.

'In fact, I'll lay odds she's already stolen from ya. It's in their genes, same as petrol-sniffing!'

'I can't believe you just said that Hillwood. How the fuck can you call a woman a fella?'

'I didn't expect you'd understand Pom, coming from England an all.'

I stepped forward and fronted Hillwood face-to-face. His watery grey eyes darted around nervously and he flinched.

'Bullshit,' I hissed before storming off.

'I want you out by the end of the month Pom!'

TWENTY-ONE.

On arrival for my first day of work at the Camelot Apartments, Stuart was all smiles and handshakes. Not knowing what else to wear, I was decked out in the togs old Bill had kindly given me; something that didn't go unnoticed.

'Good God Joseph, don't tell me you've been out all night?'

When I explained that I didn't have anything else suitable to wear, Stuart told me to follow him. Once inside his office, Stuart handed me several uniforms and told me to find one that fit best.

'So how was the wedding?' he asked as I rummaged through the pile.

I picked out a baggy shirt and baggy trousers, about three or four sizes too big.

'Oh, it was fantastic. Bit put out when I didn't get an invite to the yacht or even a kiss from the boss though.'

Stuart blushed crimson.

'Oh, really? Right…well…heh-heh, let's put you through your paces shall we?'

Put me through my paces? I didn't like the sound of that. Once I'd changed into the uniform, which made me look like an extra from a historical documentary about the Spanish Civil War, Stuart guided me around the Camelot apartments at a leisurely pace.

As we walked the corridors, explored floors, went up and down in lifts, he adopted an air of phoney professionalism, like he was working in the Waldorf Astoria or something. Well, it was my first day and I liked Stuart, so I went along with the charade but something about his persona hinted at an unseen sadness, probably something to do with getting older, losing his virility, or desirableness. I wasn't sure but everywhere we went an air of eternal regret followed him around like a sad refrain or wistful lament.

During the extended tour Stuart gave me a running commentary on the personalities and habits of some of the residents, telling me what to look out for, who to watch and how to deal with some of the more challenging residents. Outside apartment 25 - the penthouse suite - he stopped.

'Here we have what I would call a difficult customer. This is the apartment of Mrs Bird, to be addressed as Lady Bird to mere mortals such as you and I. She is a quarrelsome, cantankerous old bat, prone to tantrums and caustic comments. Of course, she was once a great beauty and prominent socialite. Think Lauren Bacall in her prime, think Grace Kelly, think Princess Margaret and if you use a little imagination, think Nicole Kidman.'

I didn't bother thinking about Nicole Kidman but thought about Grace Kelly and Lauren Bacall and immediately got a boner.

'Of course that was long ago, now she looks like your aged grandmother, or if you haven't got one, then someone else's aged grandmother.'

At that my boner went down faster than the twin towers.

'The human condition of ageing, to which we are all subject to, is no laughing matter Joseph. Lady Bird's frequent displays of bitterness are somewhat understandable, especially as she was once considered a great beauty. However, we have jobs to do and unruly behaviour by any of the residents cannot be tolerated.'

After this revelation Stuart got down to the nitty-gritty. Mrs Bird liked a tipple, in fact several each night and occasionally got roaring drunk. It was on her drinking nights that she occasionally became a problem.

'Her favourite trick is to invite members of staff into her room late at night.'

'What, for a cup of tea?' I replied with a smile.

'No, she wants someone to drink with, some company and on the odd occasion she has been known, when inebriated, to proposition male members of staff.'

'You wouldn't think they still had it in em, would ya?'

'No, well, you wouldn't; but remember if she does invite you into her room you must never, under any circumstances, go inside. If you do, it will be a case of instant dismissal.'

After the guided tour and a quick run down on a plethora of possible resident requests Stuart handed me a set of keys and went home. Just before he left, he told me there would be plenty of quiet periods and advised me to bring a book to read in future. Then, apart from a sleepy security guard, stationed just inside the main entrance, I was all alone. I sat at a small desk, put my feet up, and glanced at the apartment numbers, 25 in all; each with a tiny light bulb above. When a resident made a request, the bulb lit up and a buzzer sounded. As long as they didn't go off simultaneously the job would be a piece of piss.

For the first hour there were no requests and soon I was bored. I was allowed one free meal a night so I went to the kitchen and helped myself to a cheese sandwich and a fruit plate. The fridge was laden with plenty of ready-made food, left by the day cook in anticipation of future room service requests. There was also free tea and coffee. It didn't take me long to make myself at home. At ten-thirty I got my first request, Mrs Chilmaid in apartment 12, one glass of warm milk and a digestive biscuit.

'Coming up,' I told the elderly woman brightly.

After delivering the order, I immediately returned to my post. Again I couldn't believe my luck. This was the easiest job I'd ever had and once accustomed to night working, I was sure to be able to write and get paid for it at the same time. With this job the future didn't look so bleak, I could save money, write poetry and in a few months time take Rosie on that promised road trip to Brisbane.

Room service requests were few and uncomplicated. I took the order via the intercom, prepared the order, and delivered said order. In between orders I rested easy. Then, on the stroke of midnight, the light bulb of number 25 flashed; the apartment of the infamous Lady Bird.

Remembering the words of warning from Stuart I answered the call with some trepidation.

'Bring me a whisky and soda,' ordered a voice that sounded like a scarecrow.

No 'please' I noted.

'Would you like ice with that, Lady Bird?'

'Of course.'

Although grumpy and sounding like it had smoked a billion cigarettes the voice had class written all over it, good breeding, privilege, the voice of a confirmed snob in other words. I went to the kitchen and prepared the drink. As I poured the whiskey, I was suddenly thirsty. Drinking on duty equated to instant dismissal. And as Stuart had gone out of his way to be nice I didn't want to let him down, especially on my first night of work. I looked at all the alcohol. They had everything; beer, wine, spirits, liquors and the temptation to have a quick toot was overwhelming. Utilising all my will power I averted my gaze from the plentiful beverages and tray in hand, headed to Lady Bird's apartment.

Outside her room, I hesitated before knocking. No matter what the old hag says you must not enter her room, I told myself sternly.

I rang the doorbell and waited. I heard shuffling and grumbling, things being knocked over, curses and protestations. After an age the door opened and a frail, white haired lady, appeared. She was dressed in an old grey nightdress that was covered in stains and cigarette burns. Seconds later a powerful waft of urine assaulted my senses, causing me to lean back slightly. I closed my mouth and proffered the drink.

'Here's your whiskey and soda Lady Bird.'

'Bring it in boy and leave it on the bedside table,' croaked the old bint, who promptly shuffled away, leaving the door wide open. Fuck.

'Er, hold on Mrs Bir, I mean, Lady Bird. I'm not allowed to enter the rooms of residents.'

'Poppycock.'

'No seriously. I'll be dismissed if I do.'

Lady Bird turned around slowly like a clockwork figurine. She eyeballed me. Her eyes were a brilliant piercing blue.

'Just bring the fucking drink in boy.'

I was in a no-win situation. Fuck it, I would just have to go inside, put the drink down and then get the fuck out of there.

I took a deep breath so as not to be overpowered by the stench of two-day old piss and hurriedly placed the drink on a bed-side table. As I did, a silver-framed photograph caught my eye. The photograph showed Lady Bird in her youth, situated in an alpine location, an impressive range of snowy mountains in the back-ground.

Stuart was right she had once been an attractive woman, full of vitality, with glossy blonde hair and a glamorous smile. I did a quick one two from the photo to Lady Bird and wondered. How do people get so old? How do they change so much? How does that shit happen? But it does and it happens to each and every one of us.

'So you're the new one then?' said Lady Bird.

'Yep, this is my first night.'

'Well listen to me young boy. When I ask you do some-thing, you do it, understood?'

'Ok.'

'And if that limp-wristed faggot gives you any trouble, you tell me straight away and I'll have his saggy arse!'

I had to give it to her - the old hag had balls. I nodded and mumbled something about yes and definitely and then retreated out of the room backwards, closing the door behind me with a sense of relief.

The rest of my shift passed uneventfully. There were no fur-ther requests from the residents and I even managed an hour's shuteye. Before I knew it, like ghosts and phantoms of the early morn, the early shift staff appeared in ones and twos and it was time to go home.

On the short walk back to my hovel I reflected once more on my change in fortune. The job was a gift from the Gods and it seemed like a sign, a totem of good fortune, which shouldn't be taken for granted.

When I reached the Oakwoods, the sun was rising in the distant sky with most Sydneysiders preparing for another day of work, another day of toil, another day of life in the real world. Not for me though, I thought happily as I did a big yawn, a small fart, and opened the door and slipped inside.

TWENTY-TWO.

Sunday morning found me outside Mansions hotel at around ten to ten. I sat at a public bench, waiting and wondering. I became consumed with doubts, each new doubt usurping the old with ruthless efficiency, until I soon forgot what the first doubt was all about. What I did know was that I'd planned to meet Rosie at ten but somehow reckoned she wasn't going to show.

Bad vibes were in the air. I hadn't seen Rosie since the eve of the gay wedding, not one sighting, no contact, no psst, psst outside my window. I missed the psst, psst – a haunting sound that I spent hours expecting to hear, but which never came. Then again, I'd been working nights and sleeping during the day, so she could have been hanging around the Cross each night for all I knew.

Time passed slowly. It was a perfect day for heading to the beach; blue skies and a big yellow sun. I thought about the cool green waters of the harbour. I thought of jumping in, letting the salty liquid caress every inch of my body. Then I thought about Rosie and me lying side by side under the shade of an acacia tree, listening to the sound of the ocean, listening to leaves rustling in gentle sea breezes and the sound of waves crashing on the shore. Where the fuck was she?

As I waited, two ibis flew down from somewhere and began foraging in a dustbin to my left. I observed the ugly looking birds. Their white plumage blackened by pollution, exhaust fumes, a depressing sight. Their strange bills made me shudder; long, black curved things poking everywhere. What is it about the city and city life? Look what it does to people and even animals. It brutalises everything.

The Ibis gave me the jitters and I got up from the bench and paced the sidewalk. Where was Rosie? I glanced at the cooler bag slung over my shoulder. Inside were two bottles of wine, a Greek salad and a roast chicken. I walked to the main drag and scanned the street. Rosie was nowhere to be seen. I returned to the bench. Thankfully the ominous Ibis had moved on to scavenge somewhere else.

At ten-thirty I considered myself to have been stood up and my spirits sank to a new low. What a fucker! I hated being stood up – there was nothing worse. I couldn't even contact Rosie and give her a piece of my mind. She had no phone and I didn't even know where she lived. After debating the issue, going over the pros and cons, I decided to give Rosie until eleven to show, a full hour, just to round things up. Now I was bored. I saw the bottle shop and headed straight for it. Moments later, I was outside with a long neck of VB straight from the fridge, cooling my impatient hands.

By 11.30 the longneck was drunk and I was still waiting. What an idiot. It was obvious the stupid bitch wasn't turning up. Well fuck her. Maybe Hillwood was right; Rosie would only drag me down and make my life a misery.

In fact, I felt miserable right then, down in the dumps, a shadow of my former self. But just as I was about to give up, there she was, swaying towards me, looking bored.

As she approached, Rosie broke out into a little jog and flashed me her trademark dopey smile. I stood up and got ready to start firing accusations but just the sight of that big dopey smile made me feel good all over. And when she wrapped her arms around me and apologised for being over an hour late and was so relieved I'd waited, I could've jumped for joy. Eventually, I pulled away from the embrace. It was then I noticed the change. Her clothes were dirty and she looked rough, like she'd been up three nights in a row or something. Her face had broken out in a bad case of acne.

'Are you okay?'

'Yeah, yeah, not much sleep. Keep moving around.'

The only time I'd asked Rosie where she lived, she had been elusive, mentioning random names, random addresses and then changing the subject. The last address had been in Potts Point.

'Are ya still in Potts?'

'Na, I's left there weeks back, got a smoko?'

I fished out a packet of Mild Seven and handed her a stick.

'So where ya living now?'

'Jus crashing round friends.'

I fired her up.

'Maybe we should get a flat together.'

'Yeah, maybe.'

'Just a suggestion.'

'What bus do we catch?'

On the bus, Rosie was strangely muted and we didn't talk much. I noticed she hadn't brought any stuff for the beach, no towel or swimsuit and she smelled like day old sex. It felt like a bad idea to invite her to the beach. She was a city girl, a girl of the streets, not a beach bum. I gazed out the window at the passing scenes and felt gloomy.

We disembarked at the school of the Sacred Heart and walked towards the coastal path. Rosie stopped dead in her tracks.

'Where we going?' she asked.

I pointed to the path, a dusty natural boulevard that wound it's away through fig trees, acacia, wattle, and overhanging cliffs.

'This path leads to the beach.'

Rosie pulled me back by the arm.

'Whoa dude, youse think I'm trekking through the bush? Might be funnel webs in there.'

I grabbed Rosie by the waist and kissed her on the lips.

'Shut up, anyway you're Aboriginal. You can pretend you're on a walkabout or something.'

Rosie kicked me in the shin, causing me to squeal in pain and hop around on one leg.

'Fu-uk!'

'Don't even joke about that shit.'

It was the first time I'd mentioned Rosie's ethnicity. For some unknown reason, she never talked about the subject and as it hadn't really interested me, the fact she was a native Australian had remained unspoken.

'Look, I'm sorry but I mean, come on, it's only a coastal path. You're more likely to come across a funnel web in the Cross.'

'Really?'

'Yeah, like fuck - didn't they teach you natural history in school?'

'School? What the fuck's that?'

'You mean you never went to school?'

'Fucking a.'

On the walk Rosie led the way, every now and then glancing over her shoulder, to check that I was keeping up or still there, or that I hadn't been bitten by one of the world's most poisonous spiders.

She was acting totally blonde, squealing at the slightest contact with anything natural and stepping tentatively all the way. Not that I minded. I had a front-row view of her supple thighs and pert derriere, which swayed and sashayed in the sunlight. As beads of sweat dripped into my eyes, she appeared to float a few inches above the path in a sepia tinted dream. For a moment, I was struck by how unreal some situations can be, like how they might not be happening.

On reaching the beach, we found that it was already occupied. Dotted here and there were families; rowdy teenagers, two elderly swimmers and a dog. Despite the presence of these interlopers, I managed to find a nice shady spot under a blooming acacia tree; an ideal spot to plot up.

Rosie collapsed onto the blanket. I grabbed a chilled bottle of wine from the cooler bag and wasted no time in uncorking the fucker. The walk had worked up a thirst and I took a big hit straight from the bottle. I wiped my mouth with the back of my hand and offered it to Rosie.

'Wine for her majesty?'

'Shit, yeah.'

Pretty soon, we had polished off the first bottle and made serious inroads into the second. Then I got the chicken and salad out.

Rosie didn't eat the food but just sat their picking at it, nibbling bits and swigging the wine. I noticed she was the only Aboriginal on the beach; a casual observation that got me thinking. I hadn't seen an Aborigine on any Sydney beach at any time. I looked at Rosie. It must seem weird to be a minority in your native country, I thought but she didn't care.

With the wine inside her Rosie loosened up and returned to her playful self, laughing at the silly little things I was doing to entertain her. We lay on the blanket and kissed for a while, our tongues tasting of stale chardonnay. Then we just stared into each other's eyes, gazing at our reflections in each other's pupils and giggling. The sun shone but in the shade we were grateful recipients of solar warmth, without burning.

By the time the second bottle lay empty in the sand, I got energised and decided it was time for a swim. I grabbed Rosie by the arm.

'Hey, wass up?'

'Let's swim baby.'

Rosie dug her heels into the sand.

'Youse psycho, what about sharks?'

Sharks? Hmm, I had to admit there was a series of nets forty yards from shore protecting the sheltered cove but I thought they were there to stop speedboats and jet skis and other deadly aqua machinery.

'Yeah right.'

Rosie pointed at the net

'That's a shark net mate.'

'Exactly, so if we swim inside it we're safe.'

'Says youse.'

'Yeah, says meese, now come on; let's boogie!'

Rosie reluctantly got to her feet.

'Jeez, not that one again?'

When we got to the water I dived in and swum underwater. When I surfaced, Rosie was still loafing at the water's edge. I urged her to jump in and swim to me but she just dipped a tentative foot in the sea and beckoned for me to return with an urgent hand motion.

'What's up?' I asked.

'Don't go so far.'

'Why, it's lovely out there. So cool.'

Rosie folded her arms across her chest and pouted.

'Well, heys, I can't really swim, a?'

'Can't swim? But you're Australian! A non-swimming Australian is like an Irishman who doesn't drink Guinness; it goes against the laws of nature.'

'Well, maybes I never got taught.'

'But you guys learn how to swim in the womb.'

'Ah, shut up, youse Poms have some crazy ideas.'

'Well fuck, it doesn't matter, we can just stay here in the shallows and I'll give you a swimming lesson.'

'Really?'

'Yeah come on, jump in, I'm here to save you if you sink.'

With that, Rosie waded into the water until we were together. I got her to lie across my outstretched arms and showed her how to kick her legs and move her arms, front crawl style. With me holding her, Rosie morphed into a little child, screaming with delight and splashing everywhere.

After several lessons I stopped holding and told her to go for it. And she did; kicking her legs furiously and crashing her arms into the water. As I watched her beginner's efforts and her struggle to stay afloat, the emotion got me, right there and then. I don't know if it was the childlike movements, or the pompous Aussie kids watching and laughing, or just me being sentimental with wine but I began to cry, the tears flooding my cheeks until I was forced to plunge underwater so that Rosie wouldn't see.

When I resurfaced Rosie was nowhere in sight and I panicked. Oh God, she might drown, was my first overreaction. I dived underwater and opened my eyes but saw nothing apart from a bunch of blubbers, which I mistook for jellyfish and panicked even more. Shit, shit.

I stood up and scanned the immediate environment and then Rosie burst from the water, holding her nose and laughing hysterically.

'Ha, gots ya!'

I waded over angrily and took her in my arms. 'Don't do that again, I was scared.'

Rosie put her arms around my neck.

'You really care about me don't cha?'

I kissed her salty lips.

'Of course I do. With you by my side I feel I can do anything.'

'Shit, - kiss me then.'

And I did but when we separated I noticed something for the first time. I grabbed Rosie's arm and examined the limb closely. They were almost imperceptible, like they didn't exist in reality. A figment of imagination, a dream sequence but they were there all right, tiny and faint needle tracks. Rosie tried to pull her arm away.

'What ya's doing?'

I looked direct into her magical eyes.

'Why?'

Rosie wriggled and squirmed in an attempt to escape my hold but she wasn't going anywhere.

'Why, what?'

'You know what. Don't lie to me.'

'Let me go.'

I let go.

'Like fuck - I've only banged up a couple of times. It's no big deal.'

'No big deal? Shit Rosie, this is a big deal, this is serious, it's not a fucking game.'

'Ah, give it a rest, a?'

'No I won't fucking give it a rest, don't you see what you're getting yourself into?'

'Na.'

'Well let me explain, you're poor, the poorest of the poor, a habit is not for the likes of you, it's for doctors, lawyers and priests. And also, it's not for the likes of me. The likes of us cannot afford to cultivate a habit until we are in such a position that it won't drag us into the gutter, then we can do what we fucking like, got it?'

Rosie waded away from me.

'Get what? You're off ya fucking head!'

I followed in watery pursuit.

'Don't fucking wade away from me!'

'Fuck you.'

By now some people on the beach, noticing the argument, had begun to stare, and one blonde woman had the audacity to shake her head disapprovingly. This infuriated me and when I caught her eye I mouthed 'fuck off' - a simple act that caused the woman's jaw to drop open. Swallow a fucking fly, you stupid bitch!

Rosie was now marching across the sand. I caught up with her, grabbed her arm and spun her around.

'Listen you stupid divvy bird, I was put on this earth to be with you. We were born to be together; it's as simple as that. And you will never, ever meet anyone like me and together we will have a wonderful life.'

A steely-eyed determination appeared in Rosie's eyes.

'Let go of my fucking arm Pom.'

The word Pom pierced my heart like a well-aimed harpoon.

'What?'

'What fucking wonderful life? You're just a night porter living in a roach-infested apartment. Youse don't know shit.'

I looked from side to side, was she talking to me?

'Listen...'

Rosie stood with both hands on her skinny hips.

'No you listen to me, what are youse on? What d'ya think this is? This isn't romantic, this is stupid and you're an idiot.'

'And what's so much fucking better, I mean what would you rather be doing?'

Rosie sighed and rolled her eyes.

'Youse don't get it. All I's wanna do is, root, toot and shoot!'

I couldn't believe she'd said those words but it was a classy statement and I tried in vain to think of a suitable response.

'I'm outta here,' said Rosie.

'Fuck you, if you leave then we're over.'

'You're hopeful but I'm glad youse said it, coz I've been trying to tell ya the same shit for weeks.'

'What the fuck?'

'Your problem is ya can't see what's in front of ya fucking nose.'

If I'd had a gun I would have gladly shot the stupid bitch dead like a dog and admitted to the crime afterwards with a smirk. How could she say such things? This was me she was talking to; Joseph Ridgwell - her true love.

'But...'

'I'm going.'

'Rosie!'

I watched as she marched away. Everyone on the tiny beach engrossed in watching the spectacle. I gave them a final ineffective finger, then gathered my things and ran away. I found a huge wave - smoothed rock on the next beach along, sat down on it and gazed at the horizon.

Fuck Rosie and fuck everything. What the fuck was I playing at? There was no future with Rosie, we had nothing in common. We could never be together and it was madness to think otherwise. The thought of home and my family gate-crashed my mind and caused mayhem. Who did I think I was? I was no poet, no artist. Only people with trust funds or inmates of lunatic asylums could call themselves such flaky things. I was just an ordinary bum and I should go home, get a career and become like everyone else; a walking stiff.

Gazing upon the horizon I took in the pleasures of the harbour; a white sailing boat, the harbour bridge, even the Opera House, while tears cascaded down my cheeks in monsoon quantities.

TWENTY-THREE.

After the public row on the beach, Rosie disappeared from my life. I looked for her in the Cross, of course but she was nowhere; vanished like an apparition into the lonely void. Sometimes I wondered if I'd met her, or whether I was in Australia, or how somehow it had all been a dream and I would wake to find myself in London looking out on a cold East End morn.

So reality seemed to be a distant place and everyday without her a little piece of my heart was taken away by men in white coats for analysis. The men in white coats said my heart fragments needed to be analysed so that future generations wouldn't have to suffer like me. But in the interim, my waking hours became a living torment. Oh, where was she?

Hillwood kept it up with the threats of eviction; that cunt just wouldn't let it lie, no compassion whatsoever. Whenever I saw him he repeated the same cheesy line.

'End of the month, Pom. End of the month and you're out.'

Fuck him and his end of the month bullshit, I thought. I know my rights, I thought.

Time passed. I worked nights at the Camelot and did nothing during the day. I didn't write any poetry and I didn't think about writing any. Mostly I daydreamed about my childhood; pleasant episodes recalled fondly and I was saddened by the fact it was now impossible to ever return to that golden age. Other than that, I thought about Rosie constantly.

On top of everything else, work became a problem. The main thing was boredom. For hours on end, I had nothing to do and no one to talk to. I went for strolls around the apartments in the wee small hours, completed crosswords, had catnaps but the nights still dragged.

I took a visit to my local library and loaned a pile of books but the library was another problem. I lucked out with a battered copy of Bukowski's, The Most Beautiful Women in Town, Wu-Che-Eng-En's Monkey and A Henry Lawson Reader but those literary gems were quickly devoured and the rest of the collection was rubbish. There were thousands of tired titles by long-forgotten authors, tomes and tomes mediating on tedium, all with writing as flat as the paper it was typed on. Okay they had a few classics but I didn't want to read Dickens, Jane Austin or Tolstoy - all those dead writers. I wanted to read something modern. I wanted to read stuff written by someone like Rosie or me that related to the streets but there was nothing like that there.

There was also the little problem of Lady Bird. Every night she called down for her midnight whiskey and soda and every night, she invited me into her room. She was relentless. After a few days, I run out of excuses. Stuart's words of warning played on my mind. And then the night came when I thought fuck it, she was lonely and I was bored. What harm could it do to have one little drink with the old boot?

On the night in question, I was going out of my mind with boredom. There were no books to read, no room service requests, nothing to do. Out of desperation, I resorted to observing the movements of a little bug on my desk. But the little bug was just as bored as me; it didn't go anywhere and didn't do anything, apart from occasionally waving its tiny antenna.

Due to my acute case of writers block, I had long given up trying to write poetry but for old times sake I gave it another whirl. Funnily enough, after twenty minutes it was the same old story. The only thing I managed to write was, 'I see the sea and the sea sees me,' over and over. I couldn't even see the sea. I followed that gem with some intricate doodles, complex structures that went nowhere and meant nothing. This wasn't living, this was existing; taking tiny steps closer to the grave.

The boredom was so bad that I looked forward to Lady Bird's midnight room service request. At least it was another human voice. Slowly the hands of the clock turned to the desired position and with perfect timing, the light bulb flashed and the buzzer sounded. I picked up the intercom.

'How can I be of assistance Lady Bird?'

'Bring me my usual boy, on the double!'

'Coming right up.'

'It'd better be.'

I walked into the kitchen smiling. Even though she was a rude old goat, I admired the Bird's style. She didn't fuck around pretending to be polite and told it like it was, which is exactly what everyone else should do; fake politeness being so wearisome.

As I mixed the whiskey and soda just the way she liked it, the bottle moved to my lips and encouraged me to take a hit. This involuntary action took me by surprise. How the fuck did that happen? Was some unseen psychic force with the power to move solid bodies operating in the vicinity? Then I saw the bottle of vodka and mixed myself a large V&O. This time it was definitely me that made the drink but even so, an invisible force was doing most of the work. I polished off the V&O in two gulps and took Lady Bird her drink.

By the time I was outside her room, the alcohol had hit my bloodstream, giving me a nice warm kick. Then the door opened.

'About time boy, bring it in!'

I stepped inside, holding a shirtsleeve to my mouth to deflect the stench of two-day-old piss.

'There you go Lady Bird.'

Mrs Bird was standing in front of me, smoking a cigarette from a long black cigarette holder and leering. She took a slow, languid drag from her fag and blew out a cloud of grey smoke.

'Don't you get bored down there all by yourself?'

She was wearing the stained nightdress she always wore but now it was half undone and a glimpse of saggy breast revealed itself, deflated like a week-old balloon.

'Yes, I do.'

Lady Bird's piercing blue eyes sparkled mischievously.

'Go downstairs and fetch me the rest of the whiskey and a bottle of soda and get a six pack for yourself.'

'Ah, now hold on a minute Lady Bird, you know I'm not allowed to fraternise with any of the residents.'

'Bull dust!'

'Lady Bird, Stuart has clearly stated…'

'Double bull dust! That limp-wristed fairy will do no such thing, now get the drinks in boy.'

Somehow having a few drinks with this old bat whilst getting paid at the same time was a more than tempting proposition. Then I remembered the room service requests, the little bulbs and buzzers.

'I would like to but I have to be at my desk to answer any potential requests.'

Lady Bird flicked her cigarette holder and a column of ash dropped to the expensive shag pile carpet. She held a finger to her lips.

'Shussh!'

'What?'

'Can you hear that?'

The silence resonated. 'Hear what?'

At that the old biddie smiled, revealing pink gums and a strange, snake-like tongue.

'Exactly. All the other residents are fast asleep; unless that is, a couple have snuffed it. Now, do what you're told my boy.'

Shit and fuck. What should I do? I licked my lips, I really did fancy another drink and it was so lonely and boring at reception.

'Okay, but promise you won't say anything to Stuart.'

'That's more like it, about time you showed a little Dunkirk spirit, now get the damn drinks, you fool.'

And that was that, I got the drinks.

It all started out okay. Once she had her way, Lady Bird was entertaining company. I drank three beers to every one of her whiskey and sodas and it wasn't long before I was good and boozy.

Lady Bird regaled me with tales from the distant past. She talked of long forgotten parties, balls, functions and unremembered social events. She had never married and there were no children; too busy for all that she said but there had been plenty of lovers - all dead now of course. She had also travelled the world several times over, one of the jet set, the privileged few that never have to do a day's work in their entire life.

I sat there drinking my beers and listening. I didn't talk about myself and Lady Bird never asked. She was only interested in talking about her life; a life that was nearly over and I was more than happy to listen. Might help with my poetry, I ruminated, as Lady Bird took an extended trip down memory lane, detailing events that had occurred many decades ago with more than a wistful look in her eyes.

Then Lady Bird produced a photo album and asked me to sit next to her. There were hundreds of photos in the album; wedding photos, family photos, pictures of her in her youth.

'Wasn't I a stunner?' she asked after I'd seen some photos of her in a swimsuit, dating back to the 1930's.

I had to admit she was. Long glossy blonde hair, glamorous smile and a comely figure. It wasn't long before I was wishing we could go back in time and she would be twenty-one again and I could fuck her, right there and then.

'Yeah, I would've steamed in back in the day.'

Lady Bird made some strange clucking sounds.

'Forget it Pom, you wouldn't have stood a chance. I only entertained the crème de la crème of society, Lords, Ambassadors, Dukes, Captains of Industry.'

Cheeky fucker, I thought, although it was most undoubtedly true. Then Lady Bird licked her lips and gave me what can only be described as the sauciest of old woman looks.

'But you might be in with a chance now my boy!'

With those words I nearly spurted a mouthful of beer over Lady Bird's expensive looking photo album. Might be in with a chance now? This old hag was taking things beyond the limit.

Noticing my shocked expression Lady Bird stood up and commenced a creaky jig right in front of me. I clapped my hands and urged her on as she leaned back her ancient head and let out a, long, wheezy, cackle. Drunk with whiskey she was able to execute some nimble moves and lose twenty years in the process. Then she raised her nightie high above her knees and flashed a pair of septuagenarian thighs at me.

'I may be old boy but my pins are in still good shape, wouldn't you say?'

I blushed bright red with embarrassment but checked out her legs and had to admit that for her age they weren't bad at all, the skin was saggy but in truth I'd seen worse legs on a twenty-year old. I shielded my eyes with my hand.

'Lady Bird, please lower your dress.'

The old hag dropped her filthy night dress.

'Thought as much. A faggot.'

'Easy...'

After a moments silence the old bat ordered me to fix another whisky and soda and light another cigarette for her. Then she told me to sit down.

'Listen boy, I want to ask you something.'

I sat there wondering what was coming next, sipping my beer thoughtfully but saying nothing. Lady Bird eyed me up and down. Then she dropped the mother of all bombshells, a devastating request guaranteed to make your hair stand on end.

'I want you to fuck me.'

Blimey, this was a turn up for the books.

'Pardon?'

'Yes Pom. I'm getting old and I want one last fuck before I die.'

Double blimey, fuck a granny, now there was an interesting innovation but fucked if I was gonna do it.

'Lady Bird, please, you're embarrassing me!'

Lady Bird pointed her cigarette holder at me accusingly.

'What if the roles were reversed?'

'What?'

'If I was you and you were me?'

'That's nuts!'

'What's nuts about it? I want one last sexual experience before I depart this mortal coil, I'd say that was a completely sane desire.'

I had to admit it was a totally logical request.

'But you're not going to die, you've got years left, a decade at least.'

Lady Bird let out a series of rasping, bloodcurdling wheezes. 'Bull dust, I'm on my last legs, now will you or won't you?'

'I can't!'

'Two grand says you can.'

'What?'

Lady Bird eyeballed me with grim determination. Obviously her mind was well and truly made up on the matter.

'Two grand cash!'

Jesus Christ. What the fuck had I got myself into? But two grand was a lot of money and I only had to shag an old lady to get it, holy shit.

'Are you serious?'

'Never been more serious in my life boy!'

Now this was a great dilemma, one not to be dismissed off-hand. Two grand cash... I could do a lot with two grand in cash, take Rosie on that long promised road trip for example. But could I physically do it; could I actually stick my cock into that decrepit pussy and pump away?

'Er, give me some time to think about it.'

'Yee- ha, that's the sprit. I knew you wouldn't let me down. You've got balls boy. I knew that straight off. Now, take as long as you need because I'm not going anywhere and remember it will be our little secret.'

I glanced at my watch, it was 3AM and I was trembling with drink and amazement.

'Look I'd better get back, it's getting late.'

Lady Bird nodded like a wise old sage or some ancient eastern Brahmin.

'Okay but fix me one more whisky and soda before you leave!'

As I fixed the drink I gave Lady Bird an imaginary salute, for let it be known here and now, that old hag was hardcore to the bone.

TWENTY-FOUR

The next few days past uneventfully; sleep, work, no sign of Rosie; sleep, work and still no sign of Rosie. At work, nothing happened. After her extraordinary request Lady Bird was strangely subdued. She ordered her midnight tipple of whisky and soda like normal but no longer asked me to join her for a drink.

In a way I was relieved. It was a pressure I could do without but in the small hours, the offer weighed heavily on my mind, dominating all the other thoughts that resided there - even the Rosie ones. Had she been serious? Had she been drunk? Did she even remember her proposition or did I imagine the whole episode? To be honest, I didn't really know and wasn't sure if I cared.

Then, in walked Rosie. You returned, didn't you Rosie? You came back, like I hoped and prayed you would and when you did, you broke my heart all over again.

I was lying in bed, dreaming the dream, viewing a small patch of blue sky visible through the window, catching cloud shapes and hearing seagull cries. Then the magical sound.

'Psst, Psst!'

On hearing it, I jumped up like I'd been stung by a thousand killer African bees. The ragged yellow curtain swept aside like the piece of nothing it was. And there she was, leaning against the blackened trunk of a palm tree, smiling her dopey smile. Rosie, Rosie, Ro-ho-see!

'Can I come up?'

Of course she fucking could.

I marched downstairs, took her in my arms and she embraced me willingly. She was in terrible shape, shaking, weeping, smelling of burnt-out basements and up all-nightness.

In my room she burst into tears, a weepy soul-destroying confession that tore me to pieces. She was sorry about all the things she said on the beach, her life was out of control. She didn't know what to do - how to stop the drugs and the drinking - how to stop selling herself and get away from the streets. The only good thing in her life was me. I didn't use her. I didn't beat her. All I did was care for her. She wanted to go home.

Now I knew what needed to be done. I would fuck Lady Bird, get the two grand and get the fuck out of the Cross. Buy a cheap second hand car - a hunk of junk - and take Rosie with me. We could go to a new city; Brisbane perhaps. Start a new life, settle down and raise a family. It was a mad, crazy dream but not beyond the realms of possibility. I sat Rosie down and outlined all my plans in a calm lucid manner.

This time round she didn't mock or belittle me but listened carefully like she really believed. Could it be true? Could it really happen? She sobbed. Yes, I told her firmly, all we had to do was to hold hands and walk away.

Afterwards, I got Rosie to take a shower and she returned smelling of two-dozen red roses and as fresh as a sweet Sunday morning. I took her in my arms and we lay together, talking endlessly of future plans and far-fetched dreams.

All I needed was a week I told her. What would she do in the meantime? She would go back home to Matraville. She had relatives there and would be safe there. She gave me the address, which I wrote down: 28 Lone Pine, Soldier Settlement, Matraville. In seven days' time I would come for her and then we would start our new life together.

Rosie stayed that night, talking in her sleep, crying out strange boys' names and calling for help. I held her tight and gradually she calmed and settled. In the gloom of the room I watched her while she slept and wondered.

In the morning I took Rosie to the train station and waved her goodbye. As she sat on the carriage, exhausted by a life on the streets, she reminded me of a lost child, someone born to lose. Before disappearing out of sight I mouthed the words 'seven days' and as the train pulled slowly away she flashed her trademark dopey smile.

At work the next day something was wrong and I knew it as soon as I set foot inside the building. A bad vibe swirled the atmosphere like a venomous snake ready to pounce on its intended victim.

When Stuart asked me to accompany him to his office, I feared the worse. Once inside all was revealed. I'd been seen fraternising with residents, drinking alcohol during working hours and deserting my post for long periods. All three were a breach of discipline and Stuart had no option but to relieve me of my position.

As the charges were levelled at me I said nothing. I mean, what was there to say? I was guilty on all three counts but I wondered who had grassed me up. Had to be the security guards; there were no other suspects. The small-minded tossers.

As he revealed the bad news, Stuart's warm smile disappeared and he became stern and serious. He was disappointed, felt deflated but there was nothing he could do. His hands were tied. Then he handed me a check. I'd been paid for a full week, an act of generosity that didn't go unnoticed but only made me feel worse. Then he asked me to hand in my uniform. And that was that, I was out of a job.

Before leaving Stuart shot me a concerned glance.

'Are you going to be okay?'

'Yeah I'll be fine, look I'm sorry I let ya down but you know it gets really lonely in the night and all alone.'

'I know Joseph, I know,' said Stuart sadly.

'You know?'

'Oh yes, I did that job for fifteen years.'

Jesus Christ, fifteen years doing that soul-destroying gig - no wonder an air of eternal regret followed him around like a sad refrain or wistful lament. Fifteen years? Man that was a prison sentence.

On the way home, I did some rough calculations. There was little over a thousand dollars in my current account, four hundred in the form of a cheque, and the promise of a further two thousand if I shagged an old hag. Put together it wasn't a great deal of money but it was enough to buy a cheap second, third or even fourth hand car and get the fuck out of the Cross. All I had to do was hope Lady Bird was still up for a bit of gigolo action and then me and Rosie were out of there.

TWENTY-FIVE.

The following night, I began to itch. I was lying in bed studying the ceiling of my room when the sensations started. First it was my hands, and then it was my elbows, followed by belly, armpits, and feet. Once the itching started it sure as hell didn't stop. I checked out the itchy areas and was in for a shock. Red bumps and thin red lines were popping out all over my skin. And did they itch? Jesus, in the words of Elvis, I was itching like a man up a fuzzy tree.

Hypochondriac fears flashed through my mind as I did an excellent impression of a crazed chimpanzee. In between frenetic bouts of itching, I tried to think rationally. What could be causing the fiery itches?

Then I thought about Rosie. I must have caught something from her, something contagious, something nasty. Grotesque images of all the scummy people she associated with flashed into my brain, the lowest of the low, the dregs of society, in most people's eyes anyway.

Shit, what the fuck was I doing with trash like that and why the fuck did I want to be with her? Was I off my nut? Of course I was, but then I was in love so I had a right to be.

Then I wondered if I'd caught something from the Oakwoods. Yes, that was it. It wasn't Rosie, there were bound to be numerous infectious diseases lurking in every corner of Hillwood's roach-infested pit, especially the communal showers!

Fuck it. It didn't really matter where I'd caught it. The fact I'd caught something was bad enough and I was still itching.

After two hours of bring driven crazy by the infernal itches, there was only one thing left to do - buy a two-litre cask of rot-gut wine and drink myself into a stupor. I headed to the nearest bottle shop itching like a monkey all the way.

I awoke in the morning with the mother of all hangovers and I was still itching. I kicked the empty wine cask lying forlornly on the floor and checked my appearance in the mirror. The red sores, bumps and thin lines had increased in number, looking like some sort of allergy or extreme rash. I downed several painkillers and headed straight to the nearest GP.

I found myself in the waiting room of the surgery of a Dr Wolf. I'd been charged seventy dollars just to be seen, which I'd had to pay upfront. What a rip off. I sat and waited, feeling disconnected and itching and scratching some of the red bumps. After half an hour, my name was called. The doctor was a distinguished grey-haired chap, with eyes that seemed to say that only he could cure me.

'Now, what seems to be the problem?' he asked.

'It's these red bumps, itching all the time,' I said.

'Okay, lie down on my couch.'

I lay down and the Doctor gave me a brief examination. He prodded my body a few times and then told me to sit up.

'Acute case of scabies.'

'Scabies! Really?'

'One hundred percent certain. You could have a skin graft and have it confirmed by laboratory analysis but I'd wager my mortgage on it and the analysis is a further $150.'

'What is scabies?'

'Mite infestation. The burrows of the mite cause the intense itching you are currently experiencing.'

'Gross, how did I get it?'

'Prolonged skin-to-skin contact with a person already infested.'

Rosie. It had to be her. She was the only person I'd had any prolonged skin-to-skin contact with.

'What's the cure, Doc?'

The Doctor wrote out a prescription.

'Apply this lotion from head to toe, leave on overnight and then destroy all contaminated bedding, clothes, etc. This should rid you of the infestation within 48hrs.'

'Anything else I need to know?'

'Any sexual partners will have to go through the same process.'

TWENTY-SIX

After reading the instructions carefully, I covered myself from head to toe in a creamy substance whose active ingredient was something called liquid Malathion. Then I lay back, opened a six-pack and waited for the salve to do its job.

At some point during my prolonged cure, a letter was slipped under my door. I got up to read it. On the envelope were printed the words 'Abbo lover.' After reading the disgusting words, I tore the envelope open with trembling hands. That stinking, disgusting ruin of a human was now taking things beyond the limit of all known limits.

According to the letter, Hillwood wanted me out of the Oakwoods that very day. It went on to say I had repeatedly broken house rules, ignored numerous warnings and breached security. I was to pack my things and hand over the key to reception. My one-week's rental deposit would be returned on receipt of the room key. Fuck that cunt. Abbo lover! Who the fuck did he think he was?

I jumped into a pair of shorts and stomped downstairs. Outside Hillwood's door, I took a deep breath and pounded the door with angry fists.

Moments later, one half of the door opened and Hillwood's ugly mug appeared.

'Hey, hey, what's all the fuss?'

I shoved the envelope in his face.

'What's the meaning of this, fuck face?'

Hillwood stepped back from the door, looking nervous.

'Well yes mate, I want you out today. You've had more than enough chances to leave before now.'

'Cut the crap Hillwood. I mean... this Abbo lover shit!'

Then Hillwood did a strange thing; he told a stupid and outright lie.

'I don't know anything about that but I still want you out, and if there's any trouble I'll call the cops.'

'Bullshit Hillwood! You wrote this letter and I've a good mind to call the police myself and get you done for racism.'

'Don't threaten me Pom, I didn't write that letter, it's not my handwriting but I do know you've been working and living in my country illegally, so if anyone's calling the cops it'll be me. Now do the decent thing mate, pack your things, hand over the key and fuck off.'

These words cooled me. I contemplated my visa situation. I wasn't sure if Hillwood was guessing but the cunt was spot on. I'd been working illegally since day one and my tourist visa had expired weeks ago. To be truthful, I hadn't even thought about it; one day legal, the next day illegal - it didn't make much difference and anyway the whole world was doing it. I decided damage limitation was the best tactic.

'You're dead wrong Hillwood but I've had enough of this dump and all your fucking rules. Just make sure my $150 is here when I come down.'

Hillwood looked me up and down with a quizzical expression.

'Mate, what is that gunk ya got plastered all over ya body?'

In my anger, I'd forgotten about the anti-scabies cream coating me from head to toe. This'll give the old goat something to contemplate. Then I remembered the $150.

'Suntan Cream,' I replied enigmatically.

'Weirdo,' hissed Hillwood before slamming his door shut.

I packed fast, still fuming at the audacity of Hillwood, the slimy fucker. I had to get him back somehow. Soon my suitcase was packed and ready. Then I said goodbye to my little room where

I'd spent a brief and unproductive period of my life but which I would never, ever be able to forget.

I rapped on Hillwood's door. When he answered I demanded my $150 in no uncertain terms. Hillwood reluctantly handed over the money.

'So where ya off to next Pom?'

Why was this prick asking me a civil question when all I wanted to do was brain the cunt.

'Hawaii.'

At that, Hillwood laughed and took a sip of tea from his grimy mug. Then I made as if to leave but instead turned around.

'And guess what amigo?'

'What?'

It was then that I got it - revenge so sweet you could make a zillion candy bars from it.

'This ain't suntan cream, it's a treatment for scabies!'

Hillwood spurted a mouthful of cold tea all over himself and the hallway.

'Why, you dirty little stinking Pommie bastard!'

But I was already at the threshold.

'And now everyone in this dump, including you needs to be treated. Yeah, that's right, sticky cream from head to toe otherwise this place will be condemned by the authorities as a public health risk.'

Hillwood was left speechless; he didn't even drink his tea.

'So put that in your pipe and smoke it you old fart and remember that he who laughs last is the master.'

'Why you...' stuttered Hillwood.

But I was already gone, hot-footing into the harsh daylight of another sweltering Sydney afternoon, wandering the streets with suitcase in hand trying to think of a place to stay for the night.

TWENTY-SEVEN.

I wandered the streets of the Cross, a lonely but happy man. Come what may, Rosie would soon be by my side and we would make our way in life together.

Mercifully, the infernal itching from the scabies infestation had abated, and aside from being covered in bleeding scabs, I was in fine fettle. As I wandered the streets, my thoughts returned to Lady Bird and her scandalous offer. Could I go through with it? Could I actually perform the act? In the end, I decided that for Rosie I would do anything, even commit murder, a chilling thought that sent a cold shiver tingling down my spine.

Money was the key to the success of my plan and I had to find somewhere cheap to stay the night. I ruled out hotels as too expensive and the thought of having to converse with moronic travellers, fielding idiotic questions about where I'd been and where I was from, turned me off the idea of any Backpackers hostel.

After a while I found myself in Rushcutters Bay Marina, sitting on a harbour wall, listening to the haunting chattering and clinking of boat masts in the wind. The stars were out along with a big blue moon, which cast an elegant shimmering glade upon the water and warmed the cockles of my heart. Then I saw the cricket pitch and empty stadium. In another lifetime I'd kipped there for a few nights before getting kicked out by the caretaker. There was no caretaker around so I headed straight for it.

I unrolled my sleeping bag and lay it down on an empty bench in the main spectator stand. It was a warm night and from my improvised bed, I could view the stars shining down. It was a lovely scene and although it cost nothing at all to stay there, that old hotel had some of the best views in Sydney. That night I slept easy.

I awoke early the next morning with the sun in my face and a cool breeze blowing in my hair. What a lovely way to start the day, I thought, as I contemplated all the things that needed to be done before I could fetch Rosie.

Top of my things to do list was to call Lady Bird. Shit, just the thought of calling the cantankerous old hag made me nervous. How could I ask if she wanted to pay two grand for a shag? It sounded crazy but it had to be done.

Second on the list was the buying of wheels. Without wheels, me and Rosie were going nowhere fast. There was an underground car park in Kings Cross where travellers rendezvoused to buy and sell automobiles. I hoped to meet some gormless backpackers, preferably young, rich and clueless, with a pressing desire to offload their vehicle before leaving the country.

Before I did, however, the call had to be made. I found myself in a public payphone with Lady Bird's number in one hand and the receiver in another. I psyched myself up. Come on Ridgwell, dial that number, dial that number! Shit like that. This went on for several minutes, until in a moment of sheer recklessness I did it.

As the ring-tones sounded, my heartbeat trebled. The whole scene was crazy, absurd but unavoidable. Then the sound of Lady Bird's ancient voice spoke directly to me.

'Hello, who the hell is this?'

'It's me, Joseph.'

'Who, who?'

Things could be heard falling over, random crashes, followed by loud cursing and cussing. My anxiety levels exploded.

'Me, Joseph, the night porter.'

Lady Bird let out several strange clucking noises and emitted a prolonged wheezing cough. For one dreaded moment I thought the old girl was going to snuff it.

'Yee-ha!,' exclaimed Lady Bird with a sudden revival. 'I'm glad you called boy. I heard what happened to your job and I'm terribly sorry my boy but you know what those sticky beak security men are like, couldn't keep their goddamn mouths shut, the fools! Now how are ya my boy?'

'I'm good Lady Bird, I didn't like the job anyway but the reason I'm calling is....'

'Yes Joseph, come on... Spit it out.'

'I was wondering about that offer, you know, the two thou....'

'Oh dear me, what has old Bessie got herself into this time? Oh well my boy, you just come to my apartment tonight at midnight. Don't worry. I'll arrange it so that you can come straight up. I think you and me need to have a little chat.'

'Er, okay Lady Bird, I'll be there.'

After hanging up, I stood on the sidewalk and scratched my head. We need to have a little chat? What the fuck did that mean? Did it mean I was gonna get two grand for shagging the old bint? I wasn't sure, but it didn't sound promising.

Around midnight found me outside the Camelot Apartments. I remained in a condition of perpetual jumpiness. There were no security around and the door was unlocked. I tiptoed inside and made my way to the lift. Then I remembered something - whisky and soda. Lady Bird's favourite tipple. I went to the kitchen and fixed a tall one, taking several hits from the bottle in the process for Dutch courage.

Moments later, I was outside Lady Bird's apartment. It was then that I hesitated. What the hell was I doing? I couldn't fuck a gran. I just wasn't man enough. Then I thought of Rosie. Poor Rosie, waiting all alone in Matraville for the boy she loved to come and rescue her! Fuck it. I would just have to do the dirty deed, close my eyes and think of England.

I rapped on the door loud and hard. Movement from within, a series of wheezing coughs, the sound of an object being knocked over, then the door was open and I was hit by the wonderful stench of two- day old piss.

'Yee-ha, come in my boy, come in and put the drink on the bedside table.'

As usual, I did as told.

So there I was, sat opposite Lady Bird, wondering what the hell I was doing there, my knees doing a good impression of Elvis circa 1956! In contrast, Lady Bird was the personification of coolness, totally calm, like we were about to take high tea at the Ritz in 1935. Then she came right out with it.

'Listen my boy, I'm not going to beat around the bush - I'm going to tell you straight. I'm too old for any bedroom antics or hanky panky, and you're too young for me by about fifty years, which is quite an age gap wouldn't you say?'

I nodded, thinking grim thoughts as two thousand mental dollars flew out of the window and out of my life forever.

'Of course it is my boy but I reckon you must be in a tight spot to ask because I'm sure you weren't relishing the prospect of jumping into bed with an old crumblie like me?'

At this I blushed as red as a robin's breast.

'Oh, no Lady Bird I wouldn't, I mean....'

'Yee-ha, don't flatter me boy. I know I'm decrepit - ancient in your eyes. Hell, I can't even control my waterworks these days.'

That explains the pissy smell, I thought.

'Well, okay Lady Bird, as usual you're spot on but you see, well I don't know how to put this but I'm in a difficult...'

'Let me stop you right there my boy.'

'Pardon?'

Lady Bird took a huge gulp of her whisky and soda and pointed a bony finger at me.

'You need money right?'

'Well, ermm...'

'Bull dust! Of course you do and as it was my fault that you lost your job, I'm going to make it up to you!'

'Er...'

'Have you got a lady friend?'

'Erm, you see there's this girl...'

'Yee-ha, that's the spirit - and do you love her?'

'Yes, yes, I do, Lady Bird.'

'And you'd do anything for her?'

'She's my one and only.'

'Now I know I'm doing the right thing. Fetch my handbag boy, chop, chop, on the double.'

Lady Bird's crocodile-skin handbag lay at her feet and I leaned over and placed it into her lap. The old crone plunged a bony arm inside, pulled out a brown envelope and proffered it to me.

'Here you are boy, take it, take it.'

I took the envelope. It was of a certain weight - the sort of weight made by many notes.

'There's five grand in there boy. Consider it compensation for loss of earnings.'

Fucking hell! Five frigging grand un-fucking-believable, sail on silver girl, wake the town and tell the people.

'Oh shit, I mean thank you but I can't take it Lady Bird. It's way too much.'

'Stuff and nonsense. You're taking it my boy and that's an order. Now what are your plans?'

'We're going to Brisbane to start a new life.'

'Good for you. Go to Queensland and see a bit of the country before you grow too old.'

Yes, I was definitely dreaming, away in the land of the fairies but fucked if I wanted to wake up.

'Holy Mary, mother of Jesus, you don't know how much this means and it's fair to say you've saved my life. But how can I ever pay you back?'

Lady Bird smiled a toothless smile and let out a long wheezy cackle. Then she pointed to a sunken cheek.

'Come here my boy and give me a peck!'

Five grand for a peck on the cheek? It must be one of the world's most expensive kisses. I leapt over and planted a big smacker plum on Lady Birds shrivelled lips, just for the sheer hell of it and when I stepped back the old hag blinked her eyes a few times and let out a shrill whistle.

'I said on the cheek my boy but goddamn it, I reckon that was worth five grand.'

'I could give you another if ya like, tongues included. I'll just close my eyes and imagine you as you were as a young woman.'

At that Lady Bird cracked up, laughing and wheezing and cackling.

'Yee-ha, you've got balls boy but one's enough. Now go and get your girl and get to Brisbane you cheeky devil.'

'Thanks again Lady Bird, I'll - I mean we'll never forget your generosity!'

'Get out of here!'

TWENTY-EIGHT.

I awoke in the deserted spectator stand in high spirits and not believing my luck. Five fucking grand for a kissing an old granny on the lips! In fact, I had to check inside the envelope for the umpteenth time to make sure I hadn't dreamt the whole thing up but no, there it was, five grand in fifties and hundreds; all those pineapples and cabbages, a glorious, life-affirming sight. Now all I had to do was buy a car, pick up Rosie and then hit the road and follow the sun!

After washing in a public toilet and enjoying a large and leisurely fried breakfast in the Piccolo bar, I made my way to the underground Kings Cross Car Exchange. On the way, I passed Happy Hockers and an association of thoughts made me recall something important. My laptop! Shit - with Lady Bird's money I could afford to buy it back and once me and Rosie had settled in Brisbane, I could start writing again. And maybe this time round, I might get something done.

I walked into the pawnshop and looked around. A few junkies and desperate people were hanging around, trying to sell stolen crap or just any old crap to unscrupulous Happy Hocker employees.

I marched to the electronics sections and stood in front of a display of sorry looking second-hand gadgets. I saw my laptop: the machine I was supposed to have composed all my original and ground-breaking poetry on not so long ago.

Then I remembered how much Rosie got for the computer. $150. I checked the price tag. $350.

Unbelievable. More than a hundred percent mark-up; unless, of course, Rosie had lied. No, that was about right for a pawnshop, which, along with bankers, politicians, lawyers and big businessmen were specialists in daylight robbery.

I caught the attention of an assistant, told him I wanted to purchase the laptop and tried to barter. I didn't get anywhere. The assistant wouldn't budge. He wasn't interested and became impatient, the mercenary bastard. In the end, I got ten dollars off the asking price, ten measly fucking dollars - a budgie!

Before leaving, I got the hard-nosed assistant to power the thing up to check if it was still working. It was and my one and only Kings Cross poem was still there, safely filed away under 'My Documents.' Hey, hey, one poem - a paltry piece of verse, despite all my grand plans, schemes and designs. But if I could write one, maybe I could write two.

Next, it was straight to the car exchange to find some pampered English kids desperate to sell their car before they went home to mummy and daddy. The car exchange was an underground car park at the back of the Gazebo Hotel. The Backpackers thought they were getting good deals at the exchange but in reality, it was a captive market and the only deals being made were bad ones.

I sidled in and wandered around. I'd already made up my mind as to what sort of vehicle I wanted and how much I was prepared to pay. Once those decisions were made, all I had to do was locate my intended victims. It didn't take long.

Sitting on the bonnet of a decent looking Ford Falcon estate, were four bored looking youngsters; two girls and two boys, none older than twenty-one. They were tanned, decked out in the latest surf wear and reeked of parental money, maxed out credit cards and homesickness.

I rubbed my hands together and approached.

'Leaving Oz?' I remarked casually, giving the motor a few cursory glances.

Immediately the four kids showed interest - a good sign. One of the boys jumped off the bonnet; evidently their leader.

'Are you here to buy?' He replied in clipped English public-school boy tones.

'How much d'ya want for this hunk of junk?'

'Hunk of junk? This little beauty has taken us all the way up the East Coast and back!'

'Ow much?' I replied, aggressively.

'Er… two thou.'

At that I burst out laughing and walked off. I did two circuits of the car park, feigning interest in several other motors but always keeping a close eye on the kids. I noticed they were arguing and when I passed a third time their leader approached.

'Listen buddy, we can be flexible on the price if you're genuinely interested.'

I acted vaguely annoyed, like my precious time was being wasted.

'Okay dude, start the engine and open up the bonnet.'

'What?'

'I want to take a look at the mechanics of this here automobile.'

One of the kids started the engine, while their leader reeled off a list of added extras, camping equipment, spare fuel tanks, water bottles, survival kit, etc. I paid zero attention to that shit and pretended to be engrossed in studying the engine. I knew absolutely nothing about car mechanics but was certain that the privileged Brits knew even less.

The engine ran like a dream, purred like a kitten. I heard one of the girls moaning about how long they had been in 'this fucking black hole' - her words - and started talking nonsense.

'Carburettors going, Big End's fucked, some sprockets are missing, needs an oil change, electrics are faulty….'

The leader made a last desperate defence of the car, which I listened to with a blank expression.

'It's got six months registration, economical on fuel, new tyres, it's….'

'I'll take it off your hands for $400.'

'$400, you're surely joking.'

'Five hundred, final offer.'

Two of the girls dragged the leader away. I began to wander off, heard more arguing and seconds later the leader called me back.

'Listen, we're in a desperate hurry, flights to catch but five hundred is taking the piss.'

I said nothing.

'Okay, okay, six hundred, it's got to be worth six hundred!'

I produced my wallet and pulled out a wad of crisp Australian Lady Bird dollars. 'Five fifty?'

The leader saw the cash and hesitated. Then one of the girls, exasperated, strolled over and snatched the cash from my hand

'Let's get the fuck out of here!'

Once the deal was done and the formalities of buying a second-hand car were complete, I found myself the owner of a black Ford Falcon estate, worth at least three thousands dollars on the open market. Next stop, Matraville!

TWENTY-NINE.

After loading up the car, I took one last walk down the main Darlinghurst drag just for old time's sake. I sat in front of a switched-off El Alamein fountain and observed the scene. It's always a strange sensation leaving a place and this departure was no different to all the others. Invisible clouds of melancholia hung heavy in the brilliant sunshine. There they were, all the recognisable landmarks, the strip-clubs, bars and gift shops and all the streets I'd walked not so long ago.

But like everywhere, the Cross was changing. Strip clubs were closing down, shops going upmarket, bars disappearing and even a legalised shooting gallery. The scene was moving on. Junkies were vanishing, drunks and vagrants being rounded up and dispersed. Long-standing hotels replaced overnight by high-rise developments, luxury apartments and sterile shopping malls.

And the people moving in were different - professional-types, city workers, office drones, nine-to-fivers, lovers of cafe society and spotless sidewalks. Dead people suited to a dead city; people without soul, living, breathing automatons enslaved by the system from birth to death, and none the wiser for it.

Where do all the junkies, misfits, hookers, vagrants, crazies and drunks go when the scene moves on? To the next frontline because there's always a frontline somewhere. There's always going to be frontline people; foot soldiers, connections, fixers, dealers, pimps, ponces, prosties and new generation street kids.

So the scene moves on and places change but the ghosts of these souls still wander the lonely midnight streets, looking for a fix, a connection or even a kiss, until eternity rolls around.

None of this change mattered for Rosie and me. We were getting out with our health and our mental faculties intact, before the Cross became just another bland corner of an increasingly sterile Sydney cityscape. We were going to hit the road without once looking back and dream the dream, like all Earth's mad lovers have done before and will do forever.

Somehow, as I headed to Matraville, driving slowly through the endless Sydney suburbs, an army of doubts crept into my mind. Would Rosie be at the address, would Rosie be waiting for me, would Rosie, would Rosie, would Rosie? The doubts fought it out on the battlefields of my mind; opposing armies, violent, marauding invaders on one side and staunch defenders of the realm on the other.

I drove through some of the wealthiest suburbs in Sydney, passing mansions and immaculately manicured lawns, the nerves increasing with every mile. Rosie was never going to come away with me. The idea itself was absurd and anyway, she was sure to have succumbed to the lure of drugs, and I was embarking on a wild goose chase.

Gradually, the houses became less grandiose, the surroundings less salubrious, until eventually I was driving through what could only be described as a ghetto.

Shops were boarded up, litter flapped across pavements and the trunks of palm trees were blackened by a million car exhausts. The people looked different too - shabbily dressed, different ethnic backgrounds and lots of them hanging around doing nothing.

Then I came to the place where Rosie said she lived, the Soldier Settlement estate, looming up at me like a nightmarish vision of deprivation. I slowed the car and drove slowly along ragged streets named after WWI battles, The Somme, Armentieres, until I came to Lone Pine.

I stopped the car and gazed at the desolation spread out in each direction. Front yards like dustbowls, plastic bags hanging from telegraph poles, broken and sagging fences like fallen soldiers in a godforsaken losing battle. Gangs of kids and packs of dogs roaming weed infested streets, mangy cats slinking here and there, sheets of newspaper whirling around burnt-out cars and dilapidated townhouses.

Then I was outside number 28 - Rosie's house and in front of me was the cracked Australian dream in all its ruined beauty. A crumbling two-story shack that looked like it had been built by Rosie herself, walls filled with newspaper and a rusted carport, even a busted window frame creaking ominously in the wind.

Shit. I was well acquainted with poverty, having been poor all my life, but I'd never seen anything like this; hopelessness hanging in the air like a velvet death shroud, while just around the corner, sunny surfer girls and boys caught glittering Pacific Ocean waves at Bondi beach, without a damn care in the world.

If it wasn't third world poverty, it was close and a million miles away from the faceless politicians boast of as a cosmopolitan and prosperous, global Sydney. More fucking lies by the powers that be, but aside from the beaches and sunshine, Sydney was like any other city where the rich got rich and the poor stayed poor, just like everywhere else.

The house itself appeared empty and derelict. I listened for signs of life - kids playing, people conversing but heard nothing except the wind blowing in the dead trees. I went to the door and knocked.

It seemed like I stood on that doorstep for a lifetime, but none of it seemed real, like a dream sequence in a film, or a fourth dimension. And still I stood there. It took a while, but eventually I noticed the door was ajar.

I pushed the door open and called out, announcing my arrival. No answer. I stepped inside. The interior of the house was as desolate as the outside. I called out Rosie's name several times, but it was useless. The house hadn't been lived in for months.

I searched the place from top to bottom, going from room to room, looking for a message, a letter, a sign, anything, but there was nothing, nothing at all. It was then that I knew. Rosie was never going to meet me. It was fate, destiny, written in the stars.

Devastated by this new reality, I ran outside and jumped into the Falcon. In the Cross, Rosie had to be in the Cross. The streets had her now. Let those ragged streets have her. Let her pound those sun-baked streets until she grew old and faded away. I started the engine and drove, heading inland.

After a while vast tracts of farmland, dotted with eucalyptus trees, surrounded the road on all sides. At some point the sealed road became unsealed and clouds of rampaging brown dust appeared in my rear view mirror. Then, suddenly, the engine lost power. I checked the fuel gauge; the light flashed empty. I turned the car around and drove back the way I'd come, but I was no longer sure what way I'd come. The scenery all looked the same, the roads all looked the same, and the skies all looked the same and everything was the same.

After a couple of jerky kilometres the car rolled to an inevitable halt. For a few moments I remained in the car. Then I got out and kicked the front wheel in frustration. A strange determination to go anywhere took hold of me. I walked away from the car, on and on, turning right here and maybe left there, further and further into the nebulous haze of late afternoon. By now the sun was fading in the west and the big southern sky turned magnificent shades of gold and purple. In this enigmatic light the eucalyptus trees stood black and motionless and haunted. It was silent out there on the road, except soft winds making eerie sounds in treetops and the oppressive crunch, crunch, of my sandals on the dirt track. Maybe if I kept walking I would wake up and find none of this had happened. What is life? I asked the dust on the road, as darkness flooded the land like someone had opened a giant dam containing the night. Then a large raindrop splashed onto my cheek, followed by more raindrops. And the rain was warm and caressed me with its wetness. I stripped off and cast my clothes aside. Now I was naked and the heavens opened and the rain ran off my body in rivers. I ran away into the mad eternal night, laughing loudly, maniacally, clapping my hands and shaking my balls at the world. And the rain was now of biblical proportions, rain like the world was going to end. I couldn't see anything, but rain. I splashed around and dived into a huge puddle and lay there thinking about Rosie...

The End.

Photograph © by Amber Ace

About the Author

Joseph Ridgwell was raised in East London and is a cult figure of the literary underground both in the UK and abroad. He has published five collections of poetry, two short story collections, three novellas and one novel.

Ridgwell Stories was nominated for a 2016 Pushcart Prize and longlisted for the 2016 Saboteur awards.

A 6th collection of poetry - *Cosmic Gigantic Flywheel* - is due to be published in 2018 by Lenka Editions in Paris.

A 7th Collection of poetry - *The Beach Poems* - will be published by New York's Bottle of Smoke Press in the summer of 2018.

Ridgwell's work has also appeared in numerous anthologies.

For further details of the authors work and current state of mind go to his website: http://josephridgwelljr.wordpress.com/

COLOPHON

This second edition of *Last Days of the Cross* was published in May 2018 by Ternary Editions. Designed and typeset by Bill Roberts in North Salem, New York. The text is set in Adobe Caslon Pro.

www.ingramcontent.com/pod-product-compliance
Lightning Source LLC
Chambersburg PA
CBHW060229180626
46813CB00007B/3010